"MONTANA, WILL YOU KISS ME?"

"Good grief, Katie, what are you asking? You're playing with fire."

"I don't mean a passionate, run-for-the-hills invasion. I mean just a sharing, 'I understand' kind of kiss. Please?"

He was going to regret it. But he couldn't refuse. "This isn't smart, you know."

"Probably not. But maybe I'd like to do something that isn't smart. Maybe I'm tired of being careful. Maybe, for once, I'd like to be a little wild and crazy."

"I'm not sure I know what an 'I understand' kind of kiss is." He lowered his face until their lips were only a breath apart.

"Improvise," she whispered, reaching up, and pulled him down.

Their lips touched, lightly. He only meant to linger for a second, then pull away. But that was before he touched her and felt the shattering of his control. Eagerly she returned his kiss, parting her lips, using her tongue to draw quick little swirls on the inner lining of his mouth.

Montana tried to draw back, but she was having no part of that, and this time it was he who shifted his body so that he could touch her the way she was touching him. He still wasn't certain what an "I understand" kind of kiss was, but he knew that even if their thinking processes weren't in complete agreement, their bodies were.

WHAT ARE *LOVESWEPT* ROMANCES?

They are stories of true romance and touching emotion. We believe those two very important ingredients are constants in our highly sensual and very believable stories in the LOVE-SWEPT line. Our goal is to give you, the reader, stories of consistently high quality that may sometimes make you laugh, sometimes make you cry, but are always fresh and creative and contain many delightful surprises within their pages.

Most romance fans read an enormous number of books. Those they truly love, they keep. Others may be traded with friends and soon forgotten. We hope that each LOVESWEPT romance will be a treasure—a "keeper." We will always try to publish

LOVE STORIES YOU'LL NEVER FORGET BY AUTHORS YOU'LL ALWAYS REMEMBER

The Editors

Loveswept® 855

Mac's Angels:
SCARLET
LADY

SANDRA
CHASTAIN

BANTAM BOOKS
NEW YORK · TORONTO · LONDON · SYDNEY · AUCKLAND

MAC'S ANGELS: SCARLET LADY

A Bantam Book / October 1997

ISBN 0-553-44551-0

Published simultaneously in the United States and Canada

Bantam Books are published by Bantam Books, a division of Bantam Dou-
bleday Dell Publishing Group, Inc. Its trademark, consisting of the words
"Bantam Books" and the portrayal of a rooster, is Registered in U.S.
Patent and Trademark Office and in other countries. Marca Registrada.
Bantam Books, 1540 Broadway, New York, New York 10036.

PRINTED IN THE UNITED STATES OF AMERICA

OPM   0 9 8 7 6 5 4 3 2 1

PROLOGUE

The New Mexico mountain hideaway known as Shangri-la to its creator and Angel Central to its grateful clients, had been peaceful for weeks. Lincoln McAllister knew it was too good to last. A need would arise and an angel would be asked to return the help given to him or her.

This time the call came from Sterling, secretary and administrative assistant to Mac's old friend Conner Preston. Because of Mac, Conner had been reunited with the only woman he'd ever loved. Now they were on their honeymoon, leaving the ever-faithful Sterling in charge of Conner's firm. But this call wasn't business, it was a personal request for Mac's help.

Sterling needed an angel.

"It's Katherine Carithers," Sterling explained. "Her brother, Carson, came to see me. He's made some bad business decisions and Katie has come up with a plan to rescue him. Seems Carson's tried to recoup his losses by gambling. He lost. Then he put up his share of the family plantation as collateral for his gambling debts."

"Plantation?" Mac said with a laugh. "As in the Old South? What is this, some kind of antebellum melodrama?"

"Almost. The Caritherses go back that far. Old Carson, one of the first planters along the Mississippi, gambled on cotton and indigo. He won big. He was smart, too, put his money in foreign banks before the War Between the States. The present Carson, his great-great-great-great-grandson, just gambled—not for himself, mind you, but in a foolish effort to save that business."

"What's your connection, Sterling?" Mac asked. With every telephone call he received, Mac became more intrigued by the mysterious Sterling, who ran her boss's business empire but was never seen by the public. Though he and Sterling went back a long way, Mac had never known her to ask for a personal favor—until now.

"Katherine is the daughter of one of my mother's oldest friends. She and her husband were killed in a plane crash two years ago. The family business has already gone under, but Katherine is determined to protect the plantation and her brother. Mother says she's a certified genius when it comes to numbers."

"Okay. She's a genius with numbers."

"Oh, Mac, I'm explaining this badly. According to Carson, Katie went to a casino tonight to gamble. She expects to win enough money to pay off her brother's gambling debts and buy his marker back from the man who holds it and the plantation. I'd like to help her, but she's so proud she isn't likely to accept help, and I . . . can't leave here."

"Sounds like foolishness runs in the family."

"Carson says she's a poker whiz. But she's never played with professionals. Mac, she's convinced she can win."

"So was her brother."

Sterling gave a low, throaty laugh. "Mac, the man she's taking on is a real pro."

"Oh? Who?"

"He calls himself Montana now, but I managed to find out that his full name is—can you believe this?—Rhett Butler Montana. He owns a Mississippi riverboat casino called the *Scarlet Lady*."

Mac couldn't hold back a chuckle of his own. He'd gotten Montana a job on that boat years ago when his family had disowned him. Now he owned the boat. And he'd dropped the famous name his starstruck mother had given him. Montana suited him very well.

"Ah, Sterling. Not a world-shaking dilemma, but interesting. Is Katherine beautiful, smart, and conniving?"

"I don't know what she looks like, but she's just as determined to keep her family together and save their land as the original Scarlett. And she thinks Montana is ready to take it. Carson is worried. I said I'd see what I could do. If you can help, I'll owe you."

"Of course," Mac said. Finishing their conversation, he dropped the phone into its cradle and leaned back in his chair. "And I think we can keep the lady from knowing she's being helped."

Mac had been surprised at the emotion in the normally unruffled Sterling's voice. Gamblers who got themselves in trouble weren't Mac's idea of people with earth-shattering problems, but he couldn't ignore her request to bail the girl out, and it *was* time he checked on the man calling himself Montana.

Though if Katherine had already left for the riverboat casino, Mac was too late to stop her. Maybe losing would teach her the lesson her brother hadn't learned. Of course, she could win. Katie, Rhett Butler, and the *Scarlet Lady*.

Intriguing.

If the players were anything like their namesakes, the South could rise again. It was time he called in his marker from Montana. He tried the gambler's office. Montana was on the river. Mac left a message and sat back to wait.

While he waited he thought about the mysterious Sterling who was never more than a voice on the telephone.

ONE

A hush fell over the rowdy Saturday-night crowd of gamblers on the third deck of the Mississippi riverboat known as the *Scarlet Lady*.

The dark-eyed man, Rhett Butler Montana—Montana to his customers—glanced up, searching for the reason. The third deck was reserved for the serious gamblers, but this kind of silence meant trouble. It took one look at the woman standing in the doorway to know he'd found the reason.

Her hair was shiny black, pinned up with a swatch of red glitter and feathers. Her dress, held up by thin straps that challenged the law of gravity, had a short skirt barely covering long legs that ought to be illegal.

She simply stood, studying the scene before her with mesmerized concentration—until she spotted Montana. Then, deliberately, it seemed, she parted and moistened her lips.

"Whoa, boss," Royal Lennox whispered from his

customary position behind the cashier's booth. "Who's the lady?"

But Montana didn't answer. The connection between them was so potent he had no words. She didn't move, and neither did he. Her gaze wasn't just a question; it was a come-and-get-me dare. She was defying him to respond.

Lazily, he reached into his pocket and pulled out his signature cheroot, biting off the end and clamping it between his teeth. Then he dipped his head slightly in acknowledgment of her challenge.

Two could play whatever game she had in mind. In fact, he was counting on it.

The gamblers soon lost interest and the noise level rose once more. For another long heavy moment she continued staring, then gave a quick nod and started toward him in long graceful steps more like the slinky moves of a jungle cat than those of a woman wearing four-inch heels.

"Look out, boss, she's giving you the evil eye. A woman like that'll take your soul before you even know it's gone."

But Royal was wrong. Three steps before the woman reached Montana, she tilted her head, put a hint of a pout in her bottom lip, and gave him a nod that said they'd come out even, then moved past him and came to a stop at the change window in front of Royal.

"Yes, ma'am, Ms.?"

"Katie, just Katie," she said in a low voice. She could feel the man with the dark eyes watching.

The man inside the iron cage seemed spellbound.

"Chips"—Katie's voice was as smooth as silk, more Ivy League than Southern belle, until she added— "please?" She dipped into the purse swinging from a thin gold chain over her shoulder and pulled out two folded hundred-dollar bills that she handed to the banker.

Royal made a gallant attempt to speak, failed miserably, managing only a gulp as he slid a small stack of chips across the counter.

She turned, caught sight of Montana, then moved rapidly away. Moments later she was perched on a stool across from Montana's best blackjack dealer.

As the smoke from his cheroot drifted into the darkness overhead, the riverboat owner groaned. Two hundred dollars' worth of chips wouldn't last her long. Not long enough for him to find out more about her, coax her into having a drink with him, and whatever might follow. Reaching a decision, he directed Royal to take the dealer's place.

"Make sure she wins often enough to stick around," he told his astonished employee.

"You want me to cheat, boss?" Royal's voice came back in shocked dismay. "Really?"

Montana nodded. "If you have to."

Having Royal cheat to lose wasn't going to happen. He was a bad enough gambler to do it honestly.

As Royal relieved the dealer the puzzled man found Montana and lifted his eyebrows in question before turning over the cards.

The single blackjack player at the table turned to the slot machines, leaving the woman who called herself only Katie alone. For a moment she and Royal engaged in conversation. Royal was apparently explaining the game. Montana's worst fears were about to come true. A novice with only two hundred dollars wouldn't last long, even with Royal dealing.

But thirty minutes later the stack of chips had legitimately moved from the dealer's tray to the player's side. The woman was either the luckiest player on the boat or she was really good. In either case, his plan was working. He continued to watch for a while, then, after she made a really bad bet and somehow still won the hand, he decided she had no more idea of what she was doing than Royal. She just didn't have to deal with the same distraction.

It was time he gave her some.

Across the room, Katie Carithers moistened her lips again. This wasn't working out the way she'd planned. By now all her lipstick had to be gone. He was watching; she felt the heat of his eyes burning her back. As she won one hand after another no matter what she did, she was beginning to get nervous.

She'd come here to play poker, the game she knew. If it hadn't been for the confusion she'd felt at the encounter with Montana, she'd never have ended up playing blackjack. The dealer had to explain the rules. As far as she could tell, winning at this game was a matter of sheer luck, and the dealer obviously had none. Even her uncanny ability to count cards and remember exact sequences couldn't account for her success here: The dealer was using a machine with more than one deck.

She was steadily filling her pockets, but in the

scheme of things, this amount of money was mere chicken feed. Sooner or later she'd have to find a way to force Montana to approach her. At the same time he had to be convinced that she was a complete novice. Considering her lack of experience, that shouldn't be too hard to accomplish. Considering the skill of this blackjack dealer, though, she might have a problem.

"What about raising the limit?" she asked.

"Not without the boss's okay."

"The boss. Would that be Mr. Montana?"

"Yes, ma'am."

She leaned forward and gave the dealer her best smile. "Then ask him."

The small crowd of onlookers she'd drawn suddenly parted and the subject of their conversation appeared, taking the cards from what Katie had decided must be the worst dealer in the history of the game. She had no experience with professional gamblers, but if her brother, Carson, had gambled at this table, there was no way he could have lost a fortune.

"I'll take over, Royal."

"Then I'd like a new deck," Katie said with exaggerated self-confidence. That ought to tip him off to her lack of experience—no gambler worth his salt asked for a new deck when he was so far ahead.

"But—" Royal began.

"Of course," Montana said, cutting off his associate. He shoved the shoe holding the multiple decks of cards beneath the table and brought out a single pack of cards. In agonizingly slow movements, he peeled off the cellophane and let it drop to the floor. "I'm the owner of the

.*Scarlet Lady*." His gaze fell to the stack of chips surrounding her. "Looks like you're about to break my bank."

"Surely you don't think I'm a threat to you?"

"Depends. I think you could be."

His gaze was direct and potent. It said that as far as he was concerned, there was nobody else in the room.

"Do you always take over when your guests have a winning streak?"

"No, but then I can't remember when a player asked to raise the limits when they were already winning. That makes me anxious."

"You don't look like a man who's anxious."

"Haven't you heard? Looks can be deceiving. Sometimes a smile is a gambler's best friend."

She had to hand it to him. Nothing rattled him. Anyone named Rhett Butler Montana had to be tough.

When she came on board, she had headed for the poker tables on the third floor, thinking to get away from the slot machines and the noise. Counting the cards was easier when the atmosphere wasn't raucous.

She forced herself to lower her gaze. She'd made contact with the man she'd come here to meet more quickly than she'd planned, and now she was having doubts. If her opponent had any weakness, he certainly didn't show it. His hands were completely steady as he shuffled the cards. Only his half-mocking smile said he knew she was up to something, but just hadn't figured out what.

"Name's Montana," he said, cutting the cards and shuffling them again. "And you are?"

"A gambler," she said. "I take risks. What about you?"

He continued to shuffle. "I've been known to take a risk or two myself. What did you have in mind exactly?"

"For starters, what about upping the ante?"

He didn't answer for a moment, then nodded. "Sure. To what?"

She hadn't thought that far. Then, remembering her plan to lull him into a false sense of security, she said, "Double or nothing."

Montana didn't even blink, only his smile quirked almost imperceptibly, then disappeared. *Double or nothing?* She'd wanted him to think she was inexperienced. From the expression on his face, she knew she'd reached her goal.

"As you wish," he agreed.

She let out an inaudible sigh of relief. She'd been afraid he'd refuse her challenge. The money she'd won so far wasn't nearly enough. Not yet. Double that amount just might be a start.

The onlookers whispered among themselves curiously, then drew back. She could sympathize with their unease. It was obvious they weren't certain what was happening, but they sensed that it was something big. Apparently Montana didn't normally play.

"Would the lady in red like to cut the cards?" he asked, extending his hand across the table, his fingertips grazing hers as he opened his palm and displayed the cards. They weren't touching any longer, but they might as well have been. She could still feel his heat.

Katie's mouth went dry, and her heart started to tap-dance against her rib cage. She took in a steadying deep breath, then raised her eyes. Big mistake. Up close, what she'd thought were eyes of bottomless black were in fact a rich, dark brown dancing with flecks of gold.

"I don't think so," she said in a sultry whisper instead of the in-charge tone she'd intended to use. So? What the hell, she'd intended to confuse and conquer. Like her friend Cat had said as she helped Katie plan her strategy, she might as well go for the gold. "Deal 'em, Mr. Montana. I'm ready to play."

Their gazes met and sizzled like rainwater on a hot fire as he slid the top card off and placed it facedown in front of her, then dealt himself a card, faceup. He'd drawn a seven.

"Haven't seen you here before," he said.

"Haven't been here before."

"Why not?"

"I've heard it's a dangerous place for a woman to frequent alone."

"Oh?" he questioned, a hint of a smile at his mouth. "So what changed your mind?"

"Money, Mr. Montana. I need some and I intend to win a lot of yours."

"I like a woman who's honest about her intentions."

"I never have been any good at lying," she said.

He allowed himself a half smile. "Then you won't mind if I tell you mine?"

"Not at all."

"Good. If you win, you'll have your money. If I win, I intend to have you."

"I don't think so," she said in a voice more shaky

than she liked. "This is a gambling casino, money is the medium of exchange. You can't change the stakes in the middle of the game. Deal the cards please."

Her next card was a nine, his a ten. The dealer was showing seventeen points. Over twenty-one or under seventeen and she'd lose. Katie itched to peek at her hidden card, but making such a move would be a show of weakness or foolishness. Either characteristic would help her position. If she peeked she might even give herself away. She knew that was what he expected and maybe she wouldn't discourage that thought just yet. But a little distraction might be good.

"I'm sorry," she said, trying to add a little Southern honey to her voice as she stretched her shoulders and rearranged one shoulder strap. "All this"—she glanced around—"smoke and noise has made me thirsty. May I have something to drink?"

He countered with a glance of his own, up and down, never moving his gaze away from her. "Certainly. A glass of champagne?"

"Oh no, iced tea is more what I had in mind."

This time he didn't hold back a laugh. "Bring the lady an iced tea," he said, taking a look at his hole card. "The dealer stands."

"So do I," she echoed.

"Without looking at your hole card?" he asked.

"I told you, I'm a risk taker."

"I already knew that," he countered.

"Oh? And how is that?"

"Any woman who wears a dress without a neckline or a hem has to be."

She glanced down at the felt-covered table and said a silent thank you that the surface wasn't glass. He was right. After the first few minutes of sitting on a stool, she'd given up tugging the skirt down and the top up. Not only that but her feet hurt. Why had she tried to look like a dark-haired Dolly Parton? She'd settle for her slender five-foot-five-inch body. She'd even settle for her modest bustline. It had been Cat, her friend and employee, who'd produced the Wonderbra that gave new interest to an area of her figure that she'd always considered in need of it.

At that moment her glass of iced tea arrived. Everyone was watching her to see how the game would proceed. Taking a sip, she blinked her lashes and in her most disinterested voice said, "Shall we see who won?"

"Why not? The dealer shows seventeen points."

Katie's heart jumped up into her throat and lodged there. If she hadn't already swallowed the iced tea, it would never have gone down. "Let's see what I've got."

"My thoughts exactly," he drawled, and she knew it wasn't the card he was referring to.

Katie couldn't handle any more suspense. She reached out and flipped over the card. "A ten. Nineteen points. Looks like I came out on top."

"There are times when I like being on the bottom," Montana admitted. "I don't mind being dominated now and then—at cards," he added, the gold in his eyes twinkling merrily.

Katie was out of her league. She might be able to hold her own playing cards, but this conversation was making her crazy. She'd pushed her luck as far as she could for tonight. Even the steady riverboat seemed to be rocking beneath her feet. "I think I need some air, Mr. Montana," she said, and stood. "Thank you for taking such a personal interest in one of your customers."

"Please, drop the mister. Just call me Montana. And you haven't finished your iced tea."

"I've had enough, thank you."

"But you haven't given me a chance to get even."

"Getting even," she mused. "There is a certain amount of satisfaction in getting even."

"I agree. Why don't we talk about a rematch."

"I don't think so. But don't worry—Montana—I'll be back." She glanced down at her chips and frowned. What was she supposed to do with them?

As if he understood her confusion, Montana raised his hand, beckoning to the dealer he'd replaced. "Just join me in my quarters while Royal cashes in your chips. He'll bring your money."

"No. I can't. I'm meeting someone."

At that, he frowned and glanced quickly at the door. "Where?"

"On the dock."

He looked at his watch. "After one o'clock. I hope your date is patient—unless you plan to swim."

Damn! She hadn't thought about that. The boat left every night at midnight for a special journey upriver. A two-hour cruise had sounded just about right for her first foray into the world of gambling. She hadn't expected to have everything go so smoothly.

She hadn't worn her watch; her faithful Timex

hadn't matched her outfit. Now she tried to sound disinterested as she asked, "How long before we get back?"

"About half an hour," he lied. The truth was closer to twenty minutes, depending on the current. He'd better work fast. Taking her by the arm, he started through the crowd. "Shall we?"

Katie shrugged off his grasp. "I'd really prefer a walk on deck away from all this smoke and noise." She didn't want to be alone with him, but she couldn't afford to make him suspicious.

Katie always did her homework on any project she took on. She'd been told that women found Montana irresistible. And apparently, he treated them as he did his playing cards, shuffling them around at his whim and changing them frequently. Yes, she'd studied the man, but there were still many things about his everyday—every night—life that she didn't know.

"A walk in the moonlight sounds delightful," he said, allowing her to call the shots, this time.

Moments later she found herself leaning against the rail watching the dark waters of the Mississippi rush by. The lights of the businesses along the river twinkled in the darkness, and in the distance she could see a bridge. Overhead, a crescent moon hung precariously, looking too fragile to withstand the breeze that kicked up suddenly and flung dark clouds across its light.

"Looks like we're going to have some rain," Montana commented.

"Will it keep us from getting back on time?"

"It could." Actually—though he wouldn't tell her this—it could make their return even faster.

"Damn!"

"What's the matter, are you afraid he'll think you stood him up?"

"He?" Her alleged date was Cat, and Katie was pretty sure that if Cat could have planned the evening, she'd have gladly written this little episode right into the script. Cat thought it was time Katie discarded her books, her calculator, and her pained expression. A man like Montana would be just what a financial director and accountant like Kate needed.

"Your late date."

The wind blowing across the waves turned cool and damp. "It looks like I'll be the one doing the standing up." She crossed her arms over her chest and shivered.

Montana slid his arms out of his jacket and draped it around Katie's bare shoulders, using the collar he pulled up around her neck to turn her toward him.

She tried unsuccessfully to twist away. "No, you don't have to do this. I'll be fine."

"You wouldn't want to cool off your streak of luck, would you?"

Cool off was exactly what she needed to do. How could she have miscalculated so badly? She'd been so intent on getting on board and attracting Montana's attention that she never considered she might need to leave quickly. Her plan to win big and disappear into the night was not to be. A few hours of bravado was about all she could handle. Now she was trapped by the very man she wanted to leave intrigued while she got ready for her next attack.

"Guess you'll be my guest for a while longer,

whether you want to be or not. If you've had enough blackjack, we could share a late supper."

"No, I'm not hungry. I mean I told you . . . I came here to gamble."

"That's right, you said you wanted to win a lot of money. Maybe you'd like to change the game to one with higher stakes. What about a few private hands of poker?"

That was exactly what she'd had in mind. But now Katie didn't like the look in Montana's eyes. She'd seen it before. The last time she'd been invited to play poker, she'd been fifteen and her opponent had been a sixteen-year-old with more polish than a queen's silver. If it hadn't been for her younger brother, Carson, she might have lost more than her clothes. When Carson discovered them in the gazebo by the river, he'd defended his sister's honor with his fists. Carson lost the fight and Katie lost her poker-playing admirer.

That had been Katie's first, but it hadn't been her last high-stakes game. Back then, she'd learned not to let herself be lulled into agreement by pretty words and a challenge, and later, when she'd learned she had an uncanny ability to count the cards, she'd taught Carson to play poker and had beaten him routinely.

Tonight had been meant as a trial run, a warm-up for the big event. But it looked as if fate had taken a hand. She couldn't leave the boat, and Montana was inviting her to up the stakes. So her timetable had changed. She'd move to the next stage of her assault, make her strike tonight . . . and disappear.

She had no choice. Fate had dealt the cards.

Her answer had to be, "Yes."

The Mississippi River gambler neither nodded nor smiled. Instead he used a more disarming means of sealing their agreement.

He kissed her.

TWO

Montana's lips merely brushed hers to begin with, hesitantly, as if acquainting himself with something new, something special that he wanted to savor.

His hands left her face, where they'd moved without her even knowing, and clasped hers, pulling them up to drape around his neck. Then he settled in, drawing her lower lip between his in a nibble before slipping his tongue inside her mouth.

Katie hadn't expected this. Neither did she expect the rush of heat that swept over her or the overwhelming need she felt to get closer to him. This couldn't be. Montana was supposed to be her enemy. Knowing Carson wasn't a gambler, Montana had taken his money and his IOUs night after night, until at last her brother had put up his share of their home, Carithers' Chance, as collateral.

Montana shouldn't be kissing her. She shouldn't be

letting him. She was about to lose more than money to his charm.

But the pressure of his mouth intensified, assaulting her like the river crashing against the black dirt banks, washing away her resistance. She was being pulled out way beyond her depth. Katie closed her eyes in the mistaken belief that if she couldn't see him, she wouldn't respond. She was wrong. Not seeing only made the feelings stronger, more intense. Her body formed its own opinion on the matter, falling forward so that it contoured to his as though they'd been cut from the same mold.

There was something incredibly solid about Montana, something that said he was strong, that he'd protect her. And just for a second her lips welcomed that promise. For so long, she'd had to be the strong one. Now her strength was gone, forcing his arms to support her.

Suddenly a gust of moisture-laden air slammed into her, ripping Montana's jacket from her shoulders. The boat lurched, separating them and flinging her against the rail.

Katie lost a shoe as she slipped to the wet deck and Montana's jacket went over the side. Just as she was about to follow it under the lacy wrought-iron railing, Montana grabbed her shoulders. He slid one hand beneath her back and the other under her knees, lifting her, as the rain began in earnest.

"Hold on there, my lady in red. I'd consider you going overboard as welshing on a bet."

Katie struggled. But when a flash of lightening revealed the turbulent water below, she swallowed her protest and ducked her head under Montana's chin. She might have been a championship swimmer in college, but her medals had been won in a pool, not the angry waters of the Mississippi.

Without quite knowing how it happened, Katie found herself in Montana's living quarters—still in his arms. After a long moment he let go of her knees, allowing her body to caress his inch by inch until her feet touched the floor.

"I've lost a shoe," she murmured breathlessly.

"Silly shoes." Montana held her close with the fingers of one large hand while he picked a wet feather from her shoulder with his other. "Silly dress," he said, trailing the feather down her neck and letting it fall. "Let's lose that, too."

The feeling of a strap being pushed from her shoulder jerked her back to the present. She let out a cry of alarm and pushed him away, feeling as though she'd just walked out of the darkness and into a very bright light.

"What do you think you're doing?" she demanded.

"I'm not thinking. At this point thinking takes a definite backseat to wanting." He reached out and pulled her into his arms.

"Stop that!" She twisted her face away, moving out of the heat zone that seemed to surround Mr. Rhett Butler Montana. "Now what are you doing?"

"Kissing you again," he answered, "for starters."

"Put your hands on me once more, and I'll scream so loud that the boat will turn over from the press of people coming to my rescue."

Taking a step backward, she held out her hands, palms up, creating an invisible barrier between them. "I didn't come here for this. This definitely wasn't part of my plan."

He leaned casually against the dresser while he caught his breath, studying her. "Plan? There was no way in hell anybody could have planned this," he said. *Not even me. Certainly not me.*

Slowly, he forced himself to regain control. He'd frightened her with the unexpected flare of desire. He'd frightened himself as well. He'd damned near lost his head and all control.

No. He'd never been that overwhelmed by a woman. He'd never wanted to be, nor had he ever been so caught up in the heat of the moment that he'd overstepped his own boundaries. Not since he was eighteen. Not since Laura. Not since he'd lost the courage to love.

At seventeen, Laura'd had no more experience with love and desire than he had. It was this same kind of passion that had cost him the woman he loved, his family, and his future. But Laura had lost more. Laura had lost her sanity and finally her life.

Now, as he stepped back and took an honest look at the mystery woman in red who'd refused to give a name beyond Katie, he realized that she was no more experienced as a femme fatale than she was as a gambler.

But, dammit, she'd gotten to him, and his emotions were still churning so violently that he was having trouble handling the situation.

"I'm sorry," he said, more gruffly than he intended.

"I didn't mean to scare you. This was too fast. Let's start again."

His change to a slow, steady voice finally got through to her, and she began to look calmer, but she didn't speak. He couldn't tell whether it was because she had no answer or because she had lost her voice.

To give them both a chance to regroup and start again, he walked over to the table beside his bed and picked up the phone. "Bring up a pot of coffee," he said, looking over at her. "Unless you'd rather have something stronger?"

She shook her head, pulled her gaze from the large round bed, which was covered by a red spread, and glanced down at her bare feet. "No, coffee will be fine."

"And some sandwiches." He hung up the phone.

Katie felt something hit the boat with a muffled thud. She shivered, sliding her hands up and down her hips. "About your jacket. I seem to have lost it, along with my shoes."

"No great loss. I have a number of them, all alike. It's part of my uniform."

"Uniform?"

"Everybody expects me to look like"—he could have said "my namesake," but changed it to—"Bret Maverick or Doc Holliday. It's good for business, so I try not to disappoint them."

There was a long-drawn-out silence before the woman who'd almost gone into the river finally stopped her anxious movements and looked him full in the face.

"I guess we all wear uniforms of one kind or another, Mr. Montana. And I doubt you ever disappoint anyone you set out to please. I just don't happen to be interested in anything other than a gambling relationship."

"Too bad. I thought both relationships showed promise."

"No, I don't think so." She tucked a damp strand of hair back into the intricate coil at the base of her neck. "Gambling is the only thing I'm interested in. That's where I'm most experienced.

"And the kiss?"

He was toying with her, and she couldn't let it continue. Assuming her best business manner, she said, "I hope you understand that I don't normally fall into a stranger's arms. It was"—she attempted to justify herself—"just the storm and the excitement over winning so much of your money."

He didn't miss her emphasis on the word *your*. "As opposed to someone else's money? That sounds promising."

He cut off her protest. "Okay, forget personal for a moment. We'll have our coffee and maybe play a couple of hands of high-stake poker. It's always the sporting thing to do, give a man a chance to get even."

She glanced at the bed again. "No, I really ought to leave."

"We've already established that you can't leave until we get back to the dock. In the meantime, let's get you some dry clothes."

"That won't be necessary. The only thing wet about me is my feet. Just let me borrow a pair of your socks and a towel."

The picture of her wearing nothing but a towel and his socks made Montana swallow his words for a moment. He was saved by a timely knock on his door.

While the steward set up the coffee and cups, Montana pulled a pair of socks from his dresser and handed them to his mysterious lady in red who, taking them, quickly disappeared into the bathroom. He glanced uneasily at his watch. They'd be docking far too soon.

Inside the bathroom, Katie placed her palms flat on the mahogany vanity and dropped her head. She'd planned her strategy carefully. Her winnings were significant, more than she'd expected. Still, she knew she didn't have enough. And though she'd been warned, she hadn't planned on facing an opponent like Montana. It was his charm and her attraction to him that was the problem.

The only real competition she'd ever faced had been with her college study partner in accounting. He was the one who'd said that with her memory and special talent with numbers, she'd be a whiz at cards. He'd taught her to play poker. Once she learned to count the cards, winning had been easy. By the time she graduated, he'd moved on and she'd put her talent with numbers to work earning a living as an accountant, always expecting to help her father in the business.

Nothing had worked out as she'd planned. She'd gone to work at the hospital and Carson had gone into the business. She'd given up playing poker and Carson became a college student who gambled and partied. A gambler who lost.

The thing that hurt was that she'd been the one who

taught him how to play. How could she know that it would ruin their lives?

She heard Montana call out to her. How long had she been in here? She looked up and caught sight of herself in the mirror. The woman staring back at her was a stranger. It wasn't just that she wore a dress belonging to her best friend and secretary, Cat Boulineau. It was the glamorous upswept style and the feathers in her hair now glistening with mist from the storm. The woman in the mirror wasn't her. She was too sophisticated; the dress far too revealing. There was a wicked glint in her eyes and her skin glowed.

It couldn't be the kiss, though she still tingled. Sensory contact, that's all it was. It gave Montana a roguish, go-to-hell look and made her body feel like it wanted to go there with him.

"Are you all right?" he asked again.

"Yes, fine." She glanced around, hoping for another door. There was only an oversized porthole over the toilet. She peered out into the storm and wished she'd never come on board. "I'm coming." Quickly she peeled off her wet panty hose, then glanced around for a place to deposit them. She'd lost her purse somewhere. There was no wastebasket. The only drawer was filled with soap . . . and condoms.

He was still outside the door. "As captain of the *Scarlet Lady*, I've never had to break down my bathroom door to rescue a winner before."

Frantically, she pushed the hose to the back of the drawer and closed it, then sat down on the edge of the tub, dried her legs, and donned the black socks. They came up to her knees. "You ought to see me now, Cat," she said, thinking how horrified her secretary would be to see the ruin of her creation.

A second knock sent her scurrying out the door, straight into an intimate scene that stopped her in her tracks. A small round table had been covered with a white cloth. On it sat a pot of coffee, a platter of sandwiches, and the red purse she'd hung across her shoulders. Beside the purse was a stack of beautiful green bills and an unopened deck of cards.

"My purse."

"It got caught on the rail."

"And my money," she said in a whisper of awe. "In cash?"

Montana took an unlit cigar from his mouth and allowed that half-mocking smile to return to his lips.

"Most people prefer it, though I suggest you exchange it for a check. It'll be safer that way."

Katie could hardly contain her excitement. She wanted to count the money, but she couldn't let him know how important it was.

"Sit down," he said, pulling out one of the wrought-iron bistro chairs from the table.

She looked around hesitantly for a moment, then followed his directions. Though the storm seemed to be lessening, diminishing the danger of a crash, she knew she was caught up in a more intense situation inside Montana's suite. They were headed for a collision. Having coffee would fill the time and she'd have the table between them.

"I'll take mine with cream and artificial sweetener," she said.

Cream and artificial sweetener? A contradiction. Much like the lady he was looking at, he was deciding. Montana poured the coffee, adding the requested ingredients, and handed her a cup.

As she sipped the hot beverage she tried not to look at the bed. It seemed to loom larger and larger every time she did. She also avoided looking at the stack of money. Instead, she focused on the unopened deck of cards. Did he actually plan to continue their gambling?

Luck had been in her corner so far, but now she needed a way out, a way to get off the boat and plan her next move. Another casino, perhaps. In the casino, the presence of the other players somehow would act to defuse the powerful effect he had on her. Here, Katie wasn't certain she could concentrate. She needed money, but it didn't have to be Montana's money, she reasoned. He was too dangerous to her peace of mind. No, she decided firmly. It was Montana who'd taken Carson's money. It was Montana who'd give it back. Getting even, wasn't that what he'd called it?

She looked up at the man across the table from her. He seemed amused, almost smug, as if he knew all her secrets. But he couldn't know who she really was or why she was here. She'd never been to the casino. She'd never even been down the river to Silver City, Louisiana, before. And she'd certainly never gone out dressed in a way that made her very appearance an open invitation to intimacy. *She'd tell him who she was—eventually. But for now she'd remain anonymous.*

"You know I let you win," he said. "I think you owe me a rematch for my money."

She frowned. "Let me win? I don't think so, Mr. Montana."

"But you're not sure, are you? I think you're going to have to prove it. Play me one last hand as you suggested before, final bet, double or nothing."

Katie moistened her lips. Here it was—what she wanted—as Carson would say, the whole enchilada. Was Montana telling the truth? Had he let her win? No, she didn't believe that. She'd beaten him, fair and square.

"Let me make sure I understand. If I win, you'll double whatever is in the pot?"

He nodded. "And if I win?"

She hadn't thought about that possibility. "That isn't going to happen." She closed her eyes and said a desperate prayer. If she lost, she'd lose all the money she'd won, and then there'd be no way she could keep playing.

Would it matter? If she didn't find the money to settle Carson's IOUs, Rhett Butler Montana would own half of Carithers' Chance. If she couldn't make up for her loss, he'd end up winning the other half. She had no choice; she'd tried every way she could find to raise the money—without success. Carithers' Chance was too big a gamble for anybody except Montana to risk.

"You won't win," she said, and reached for her purse. "But this time we play with my cards and I deal."

"Don't you know you aren't allowed to bring your own cards into a casino?"

"What's the matter? Are you scared?"

"Scared? No. But why should I take that kind of chance?"

"Because, Mr. Montana, those are my terms."

He conceded with a laugh. "Why not? What's the game?"

She peeled the cellophane from her deck and shuffled the cards while she was considering the odds. "One hand, right?"

"One hand." If he agreed to more, they'd be back at the dock by then, and he wanted this settled while she was still on his turf.

"Stud poker."

"Fine." His penetrating gaze held hers and she didn't think he'd even blinked. Intimidation, she decided. He figured he could spook her into making a mistake. Well, he was wrong. She could be just as cool.

"Would you like to cut the cards?" she asked.

He shook his head, stood, and moved toward the bed. Another intimidating ploy, she thought. Just like his uniform. Obviously, the gambler played his part to the hilt. All he needed was a brass chandelier and gold pull cords to open the curtains behind. Everything about the *Scarlet Lady* was larger than life, including the oversized portholes.

Katie forced her expression to remain unemotional as Montana reached into a drawer in the bedside table and casually pulled out several packets of bills.

As he took his seat at the table, Katie leaned forward, for the first time intentionally using her revealing neckline to distract her opponent.

He studied the view she presented, leaned back, and smiled. "Deal."

"About the bet. One hand, right?"

"One hand."

She dealt him his first card, facedown. Then one to herself. The bets started small. The next card was faceup. A queen of spades to Montana, a king of hearts to herself. Montana made no attempt to examine his hole card; instead, he peeled off ten thousand dollars, pushed it forward, and waited.

"Is that all?" Katie asked airily, saying a silent prayer that he was the one who'd have to double the bet. "I like a man who takes a risk."

"I like a woman who matches it."

Katie silently fretted and considered her king of hearts. She would rather not have had to risk so much of her purse, but she couldn't stop now. She covered his bet and added more. His third card—faceup—was a four of diamonds; hers a jack of hearts.

"Possible royal flush for the dealer," she observed calmly. "Will you bet?"

"You know it, mystery lady." Another stack of bills was added to the pile.

She matched it and dealt each of them another card. Montana drew a second four—of hearts this time. "One pair showing." Her card was the ace of hearts. Without ever touching the cards, Montana shoved more money into the pot. With a lump in her throat, Katie said, "Possible royal flush still working."

"Maybe." Montana smiled. "Then again, maybe not.

I already have a pair. Perhaps you'd prefer to give up and save some of your winnings for another day?"

Silently Katie matched his stack of bills. When the next card she dealt him turned out to be the queen of diamonds, she blanched. "Fours and queens, possible full house," she managed to say, and turned over her last card. The ten of hearts.

Could it be? She had the ten, jack, king, and ace of hearts showing. No matter how cool she tried to be, she had to look at her last card. She just couldn't give it away . . . or maybe she could. What if she pretended to be flustered, gave the appearance of having failed to complete the royal flush? Could she pull it off?

She had to. Carefully, she lifted the corner of the card. A bit, then more, holding her breath as she looked. It couldn't be. But it was. The queen of hearts was her hidden card.

Deliberately, she moistened her lips and swallowed hard. Then she jutted her chin forward and said, "Royal flush still working. Are you ready to throw in your cards, Mr. Montana?"

"Not in this lifetime, darling. What about you?"

"How big a risk taker are you?" she asked.

"The sky's the limit, except I don't own it. Instead, I think I'll just raise you."

She took a deep breath. He was so sure of himself that he wasn't even going to look at his other card. She'd come here with two hundred-dollar bills. The pot was somewhere close to twenty thousand dollars now and they both knew she couldn't cover his last bet. She was going to lose. Desperately, she tried to come up with an answer. She had to call his bluff. For once in her life she had to take the risk. "You see that I'm a little short. What about a new wager?"

"Only if I choose the stakes."

"I'm listening. What do you have in mind?"

He studied her for a long moment. "Like I said, if I win, I get you for the night."

She gaped at him.

"But . . . but that's not . . ."

"You wanted to play double or nothing. If you win, you get the pot. Come on, this is what you came for, isn't it? You said you wanted to win a lot of money—my money."

He was right. She wanted—no, needed—a lot of money. But even double the pot wouldn't really be enough. She had to have more. "All right. But let's talk about the stakes."

He laughed lightly. "I'm listening."

She thought about what she wanted. She couldn't bring herself to say Carson's IOUs. She could take care of that later, with her winnings. What she wanted to do was teach Mr. Go-to-hell, Sure-of-Himself Montana a lesson in loss. Then it came to her.

"A night with me is worth more than this pot, Mr. Montana."

He grinned. "All right. Put a price on your services."

She curled her lips into a smile, leaned forward, and whispered, "If I win, I get the *Scarlet Lady*—and double the pot."

He stood up and walked toward the porthole, glancing out. He could see the lights of the city coming into view. He was almost out of time.

"What's the matter?" she asked, worried now that he'd back out. "A successful gambler like you is afraid I'll win?" She allowed her hands to flutter nervously. "What would people say? I tell you what, you just give up. I'll take the original bet and you get to keep your boat."

So she wanted to back down, he mused. He wasn't certain he trusted her, but, hell, he was the gambler. He'd won *Scarlet* once, he wasn't going to lose her now. "How do I know I can trust you, my lady in red?"

"Because I say so."

"A little demonstration of good faith is in order."

"Oh? And what would you consider a demonstration?"

He walked back toward her and held out his hand. "A kiss freely given, totally committed."

"But that's crazy."

"I don't think so. I'm a gambler and I'm gambling that you don't have the queen in the hole. If you do, just consider the kiss as a consolation prize."

She allowed him to draw her to her feet, trying desperately to figure a way out of the impossible situation she'd gotten herself into. Whatever had made her think she could do this? She was an accountant, not a gambler. Her stock-in-trade was logic, not odds. Her heart was pounding so, she could hardly speak. If he kissed her she'd . . . What was she thinking? She was about to win his money and his boat.

To do that she had to let him kiss her.

His mouth descended. Her heart was thudding, she was caught in his arms like a butterfly in a spiderweb. Neither one of them could escape.

And then his lips met hers, expertly, masterfully. This time she didn't close her eyes. She put her arms behind her, bracing herself against the table, feeling the crinkle of the bills beneath her fingertips.

Money.

With a prayer for divine guidance, she parted her lips and allowed his tongue to enter her mouth, using every trick she'd ever read about in a book or seen in a movie to hold his attention. She was on his boat, in his territory. She wasn't taking any chances that he'd find a way to back out of their bet. Another kiss and she'd lose more than that bet. Behind her she found her purse, opened it, and slid all the money inside. Forget the boat for now. She'd settle for the cash. She'd think about the rest of the bet tomorrow.

Finally, face flushed and, in spite of her attempt not to respond, eyelids heavy with desire, she pushed Montana away. She had to escape while he was still caught up in the moment. And before she herself was lost in the power of his attraction. "What will you do if I win?" she asked breathlessly.

"You won't," he said, his eyes boring into hers, his fingertips digging into her arms. "One way or another, I always win."

"You're right," she said, suddenly afraid of the potential for big-time trouble. "I was bluffing. You win. You win me. But first I have to—I mean I should—I mean, please excuse me." She pulled herself out of his reach and stumbled toward the bathroom. "I'll be right back," she promised.

And I'll be ready for whatever you have planned next, he thought in anticipation. She'd been a reasonably good poker player, but no beginner's luck was going to beat two pairs. And she was terrible at bluffing. Still, he hadn't expected her to concede so easily. But she had. Why didn't he feel good about it? Had he been so swept away with his lady in red that he'd missed something?

The rocking of the boat had gradually lessened. They were coming to the dock. The riverboat whistle blared out, announcing that they were about to tie up. Montana heard water begin to run. A bath? That surprised him. He moved from the card table to the bed, drawing back the spread. Next he adjusted the lights, leaving just enough to see without being obvious.

The sound of water continued while Montana ordered a bottle of champagne on ice. Still the water ran. His lady in red was taking a very long time to make herself ready to pay up on her bet.

Finally he felt a flicker of concern. Everything was too quiet. Something wasn't right. He knocked on the bathroom door, lightly, then more firmly. "Hello?"

No answer. Except now water was seeping out from under the door.

Seconds later the door was hanging from its hinges and Montana was standing inside a flooded empty bathroom studying the porthole glass swinging in time with the movement of the boat.

"Damn!" She'd managed to stand on the toilet and

crawl out through the open window. She hadn't even said good-bye.

But she had. Scrawled on the mirror in lipstick as red as the dress she'd worn were the words SORRY. YOU LOSE! Below the message was the imprint of her lips and a red feather held on by a sliver of water-softened soap.

Montana whirled around and headed back to the table. He hadn't noticed before, but all the money was gone. Finally, he turned over her last card.

The queen of hearts.

She'd won his money and his boat and he didn't even know her name. Why had she run?

It was then that he felt the tiny, almost imperceptible nick in the corner of the card.

Card by card, he examined the rest, and swore. If he'd touched the cards he'd have known. But she'd been the dealer. If he'd touched the cards, he would have known that the deck was marked.

His lady in red had cheated.

THREE

Thanks to the river's swift current brought on by the storm, Katie was going to make it to shore. With the boat whistle announcing the arrival of the *Scarlet Lady*, she increased her strokes and pushed the last few feet to the pier. Thank God for competitive swimming.

Watching with an incredulous stare from the dock was Cat, who'd helped her orchestrate the evening.

"So," Cat called out, "why the midnight swim? Did he throw you overboard?"

Katie took hold of the centuries-old iron ladder to the wharf and leaned against it to catch her breath. "No, I jumped before he could."

"Does that mean you lost?"

"No, I didn't lose," Katie answered, grabbing the bulging evening purse, still swinging from her neck, as if it were a life vest and she were going down for the third time. "Oh, Cat. I won. I actually won."

"I don't understand." Cat leaned down and took Katie's hand, pulling her up the last rung of the ladder.

"I won big," Katie repeated, her lips beginning to chatter, not from cold, but from delayed shock. She swept her hair from her eyes, captured the last of the feathers in her fingers, and flung them to the dock. "Well, it's not enough to pay off everything, but it's a start."

Cat looked down at Katie's feet and shook her head. "I can understand why you lost the shoes, but the reason for your socks escapes me entirely."

Katie looked down at her feet, still encased in Montana's black socks. "I don't think I want to explain."

"I can believe that." Cat removed the fringed shawl she'd tied around her waist as a skirt and placed it around Katie's shoulders. "What I'm waiting to hear is why you jumped overboard and ruined my dress."

Another whistle reminded Katie that the riverboat— and the man who'd kissed her—was about to dock, not two hundred yards from where she and Cat stood.

"The car, Cat. Where's the car?"

"Right where we left it, in the parking area behind the restaurant. Though if you're lucky, someone stole it."

Katie turned to check the river. The *Scarlet Lady* came alongside the pier and snuggled into her berth with a thud. Katie let out the breath she'd been holding and shivered violently. "If it's gone, I'm dead."

Thank goodness, the riverboat had been forced to slow down to maneuver itself into its proper mooring. Even so, it had caught up with her. Now anybody looking from its decks couldn't miss a waterlogged brunette in a skirt that was way beyond short. If she didn't attract attention, the red-haired Cat, who now wore only her black spandex suit, wouldn't be missed.

"So?" Cat prompted. "Tell me everything."

"I think I'd better tell you later."

"Hey! You, my lady in red!" The voice was angry. The voice was familiar and it was too close.

Katie glanced up to the lacy-railed private deck on the third level, just outside Montana's cabin. In one moment he was standing there; in the next he saw her, whirled, and disappeared inside.

"Cat, hurry!" Katie ran down the dock, cut through the now empty tourist shopping area, and headed for the car they'd parked there three hours ago. If she hadn't already lost her shoes, she would have now in her haste to get away.

She knew Montana had to get down to the dock level, wait for the doors to be opened, and fight his way through the crowd. Then he'd have to take the escalator down to the ground level and find her. Maybe, just maybe, she'd escape. If not, she didn't want to think what might happen.

One night of gambling had taught her she was no professional cardplayer. She'd never lacked for courage, unless she was dealing with her brother—or the aftermath of one of his problems. Then, as always, she turned into a first-class wimp—except for tonight, when she'd shored up her courage, let Cat remake her into some femme fatale, and come to the casino to gamble. And she'd pulled it off, until the last hand. A real pro would have faced down Montana and claimed his boat. A real pro wouldn't have let one kiss turn her into a woman running for her life. But she wasn't a real pro, and after that kiss she wasn't about to take a chance on another.

If the look on Montana's face staring down at her from the upper deck didn't tell her she'd been wise to leave when she did, the thudding of her heart was the clincher.

"You drive, Cat. I'll wreck us for sure."

Moments later Katie realized how really rattled she was. Cat was the worst driver in the history of Louisiana. She only knew two speeds, faster than a speeding bullet and dead stop. *Dead.* That might be the word of choice, Katie decided as her daredevil friend took the corners on two wheels, leaving the river and the *Scarlet Lady* behind in the wake of their dramatic exit.

"Slow down, Cat!" she yelled. "We got away."

A few blocks later Cat pulled the car over, took her foot off the gas, and looked at Katie. "All right, girlfriend. Now tell me, who did we get away from?"

"Didn't you see him?"

"You mean the devil in the black frock coat who was yelling at you? Who was he?"

"Rhett Butler Montana."

Cat let out a disbelieving laugh. "You've got to be kidding. Montana. Rhett Butler Montana. Who was his mother, a Southern belle or a cowgirl wannabe?"

"I don't know. But she named him right. He's . . . well, he's certainly straight off a western-movie set."

"Am I to understand he's the bad guy and we just got out of Dodge?"

"Pretty much."

Cat gave her a long, serious look. "One question, Miss Kitty, did you cheat?"

Katie's eyes widened. "Me? Cheat? Have you ever, in your entire life, known me to cheat?"

"Silly me. Of course not, Miss Go-by-the-Rules Carithers," Cat admitted. "But you've got a blind spot a mile wide as far as your brother Carson is concerned, and I'm never positive you won't do something really dumb to rescue him."

"I'm not rescuing him this time, Cat. I'm saving Carithers' Chance. The plantation has been in my family since before the War Between the States."

"Well, I do declare. 'Course you are. What I want to know is what your low-down, no-good brother is doing to help? The one who put up his share of the plantation to cover his gambling debts."

Katie took a deep breath. "I . . . I'm not quite sure. When I left he said he was going to get in touch with a friend, something about one last possibility of making things right. He really regrets his gambling, Cat. He just got desperate."

Cat took Katie's hand and squeezed it. "I'm sorry, Katie. I don't mean to make light of your problem, but Carson just makes me so mad. You're the one with the steel-trap mind. You're the one who should have been running Carithers Shipping, not him. If your *daddy* hadn't been a bigger idiot than Carson, he wouldn't have been so caught up in tradition. He should have left the company to the kid with the brains instead of his only son."

"He wasn't an idiot, Cat. He was brought up to believe in tradition and family—the Carithers's curse."

"And you're going to keep right on with the tradition, wasting what money you just won on that leaky ghost bucket of a house you live in instead of using it to buy yourself a future."

Katie nodded. "Carithers' Chance *is* my future."

"I'd say it's more like your past."

"Maybe, but I can't give it up without a fight. I didn't do anything to stop Carson before he'd lost the business, but I'm determined to save our home. Even if I have to take on the Old West to do it. Let's go home, Cat. I want to count my winnings and plan my next move."

"You mean you're going to do this again?"

"I don't know. It depends on how much money I have."

Cat put the car in gear and gunned the engine. The ancient sedan shuddered, then leaped forward again, eating up chunks of the dark River Road.

"Take it easy," Katie admonished. "This car isn't used to being abused."

"It's a good thing a real posse isn't after us. I told you we should have taken my Mustang."

"I didn't want to stand out," Katie said wearily. Now that they'd gotten away, the enormity of what she'd done came crashing down on her. She'd actually gone on board the *Scarlet Lady* and taken on the man she'd come to think of as her archenemy, the man known as Montana.

She'd gambled.

And she'd won—bigger than she'd dreamed of winning.

No, not her, the lady in red she'd become for one night. But now she'd left her behind, and Katie Carithers, the accountant, was back.

And as the accountant, she had to count her winnings and see if they had enough for Carson to redeem his IOUs. But first, she had to get home, and the flashing lights that suddenly appeared behind them was about to make that impossible.

"Ah, Cat, look what you've done."

"Cripes! The cops. Want me to outrun them?"

"No! Of course not. I just don't know how I'm going to explain why I'm wearing men's socks and am soaking wet."

"So don't say anything. I'm driving. I'm the one they'll give the ticket to. It won't be my first."

Cat brought the car to a stop. The police cruiser rolled in behind them, and with the red-and-blue strobes still flashing, the door opened and the tall shape of a man appeared in the light.

"All right, ladies, where are you going in such a hurry?"

Cat let down the window and was about to speak when Katie opened her door and stepped out. She couldn't let Cat take the blame for something she'd caused.

"Please, Officer, it wasn't my friend's fault."

"Oh, and why is that?"

"You see, it was storming and I—I fell into the river and she rescued me."

The driver shone his light into the car, playing it around, then moved around the car to meet Katie, momentarily taken aback by the obvious truth of her story. "Are you okay, ma'am?"

"Yes, except I'm a bit cold."

He made a motion to take off his jacket, but Katie stopped him. "No, that's all right. My friend was just overly concerned about me. She didn't realize how fast she was going. Once I get home, I'll be fine."

"If you're sure." He helped Katie back into the car and closed her door, then walked slowly around the front of the car and leaned down into the open window. "I'll let you go with a warning this time," he said. "Just watch your speed."

"Sure thing," Cat agreed, patted the officer on the arm, and drove away, leaving the uniformed man in her graveled wake.

"That helpless approach works every time, Katie, my girl," Cat said with an approving laugh. "Maybe I'll keep you around. If you aren't going to give me a raise, at least you'd save me a pile of money."

Katie shivered. She really was getting cold, either that or her nervous system was collapsing, one cell at a time.

"Not," she said through chattering teeth, "if I have to jump back in the river first."

❖————————❖

"We've had some desperate losers, but never one who went overboard," Royal said.

Montana stood looking at the water, twirling an unlit cheroot in his fingertips. "She had a royal flush. The queen of hearts was her hole card."

Royal stared at his boss, his mouth hanging open. "You mean she beat you? Then I sure can't figure out why she jumped in the river."

"I think I can."

"She must be a fool or a fish. You say she made it to shore?"

"I saw her."

"She could have drowned."

Montana chewed on the end of his unlit cigar. "I don't think she's a fool. Desperate is more like it."

"What do you mean?"

"She came on this boat determined to win a lot of money. No, what she said was a lot of *my* money. That's the key. *My* money. Why would that be?"

"You're convenient?" Royal offered.

"There are three gambling paddleboats along this stretch of the Mississippi. Why mine?" And why, he wondered, did she leave without claiming the *Scarlet Lady*?

Royal smiled. "Boss, more than half the gamblers on this boat are women, women who come here because of you."

"Women make up more than half the gamblers in all casinos, Royal." He carried on the conversation with Royal, but his mind wasn't on the words.

"But on the other boats they don't move from floor to floor when you do."

Montana looked at Royal in surprise. "I hadn't noticed."

" 'Course you haven't. You just dress in those black clothes because you like pretending you're one of the Earp gang."

"Only when I'm working. When I'm not, I look like a beach bum, which I'm going to be in real life if our ship jumper comes back and claims the *Lady*."

"What do you mean, claims the *Lady*?"

Montana pitched the cigar overboard and leaned forward, resting his arms on the rail. "That was the bet. If I won, I won her for the night."

"And if she won?"

"She got the *Scarlet Lady*. I'm sure she knows I never welsh on a bet. I expect she'll be back."

Royal frowned. Behind them, the workers were leaving for the evening, the crew was tying the boat down for the night, and the lights on the dock were going out, one by one.

"You say she won?"

"No, she said she won. She had the queen all right."

"Then I'm back to square one. Why'd she climb out the window and go overboard?"

"Because, my friend, to win, the lady cheated. And there's only one thing I hate more than a welsher—a cheater."

The message was waiting for Montana in his office, a message he'd expected for a long time. A message he couldn't ignore. *Call Lincoln McAllister as soon as possible.*

He glanced at his watch. Louisiana time was after three in the morning. But Mac and Shangri-la were in New Mexico, a one-hour difference, and the word was that Mac never slept. Montana picked up the phone.

One ring. "Yes?"

Montana remembered the voice well. "It's Montana," he said. "What's wrong?"

"You tell me," was Mac's curious reply. "Do you know a kid named Carson Carithers?"

"Unfortunately, yes."

"He owes you money?"

Montana groaned. Carson Carithers was the world's worst poker player and he drank too much. The kid was a problem Montana tried to dodge. He'd done everything but ban him from the boat. Still he came back, desperately determined to recoup his losses. Finally, Montana decided that Carson was better off gambling on the *Lady* than somewhere else. At least Montana wouldn't deliberately take advantage of his obvious addiction.

"Does he owe me money?" Montana finally said. "He does. Too much money. I'm holding a fistful of IOUs with his family home as collateral."

"And that's why I'm calling. Carson Carithers is what's wrong. He has a sister who is devoted to him. He's already lost the family business and now they're about to lose the family home. They need help, Montana. I need you to help them."

Montana wanted to swear. He wanted to hang up the phone and pretend the call had never come. Hell, if he were wishing, he'd wish the entire evening hadn't happened, including his lady in red—the lady who'd disappeared before he could get to her.

He'd learned a few things about her. She hadn't drowned. She had an accomplice. She was a cheat, a liar, and she could swim like a fish.

And kiss like an innocent.

And make his pulse quicken at the thought of kissing her again.

"Montana? Are you still there?"

"I'm here."

"I assume if you're holding his markers, you have an address."

"I know where he lives, in a dilapidated plantation upriver. But I've never been there socially. I'm a Mississippi riverboat gambler, remember. I don't get many invitations to hobnob with society."

"Well, here's your chance. A little culture might be good for you."

"So, what do you want me to do?"

"Go talk to the sister, Katherine. Someone has to take Carson in hand, someone who isn't family."

Go and visit Katherine Carithers, just what he needed.

"Montana, are you listening?" Mac asked, interrupting the gambler's grumbling.

"I'm listening. You want me to forgive his debts?" That wasn't something he was happy about, but he owed Mac—anything he asked.

"No. I was asked to help him and his sister. Now I'm asking you to do for someone else what I once did for you."

"You want me to give him a job?"

"I'll leave the details up to you."

"Consider it done," Montana answered. "I'll get back to you."

He hung up the phone. The lady in red would have to wait. His obligation to Mac came first. First thing tomorrow, he'd head for Carithers' Chance. Some name for a plantation. He'd heard young Carson brag about his home so often that he'd once driven by to see it.

"Built before the War Between the States," Carson would say, not in pride but in a mocking voice. "By the first Carson Carithers, a man of vision who took a chance and raised the best cotton in Louisiana."

Taking a chance seemed to be the one trait the present-day Carson had inherited. That and the name. He wondered about the sister. But mainly he wondered what he could do about a kid hell-bent on self-destruction.

Rhett Butler Montana had spent years cursing families who held their reputation and their traditions as the most important thing in life, who hurt and punished in the name of honor. He'd decided long ago that being responsible for himself was the only thing that mattered. A family's expectations only brought pain, and he had no intention of ever subjecting himself to that again.

Now, come morning, he was headed for Carithers' Chance and the very thing he'd avoided—a woman who apparently believed in the one thing Montana refused to believe in—unconditional commitment to family.

It was very late when Carson returned to Carithers' Chance, surprisingly sober and contrite.

Katie met him at the door. She had trouble believing that the tall, dramatic-looking man with the poetic eyes was her younger brother. Growing up, she'd always thought he was meant to be a Byron or Shelley. But he'd given up on using his creative talents when their father died and left him in charge of a dwindling shipping business. Barges weren't glamorous, and over time they were less and less profitable. And though Carson was never a businessman, he wouldn't let Katie have any more say in the business than her father had.

"Where have you been, Carson?"

"I flew to Philadelphia to see mother's friend Sterling. You remember, she's the secretary in that import-export firm, the one who works for that millionaire, Conner Preston."

Katie gasped. "Sterling? Why?"

"I thought she might be able to help?"

"You tried to borrow money from Sterling?" As soon as she let the accusation fly, she regretted it. The wince on Carson's face was too familiar. She'd seen it often when she'd reacted negatively to his decisions.

"No, Katie. Though I wouldn't be too proud to ask for a loan if I thought she had enough money to bail us out."

"Then what did you ask for?"

"It doesn't matter. It didn't work. I just wanted to stop you from going out gambling tonight."

"How did you know what I was doing?"

"I heard you talking to Cat. I knew you'd lose. Don't worry. I'm not going to rake you over the coals for doing the same thing I've done. I'm going to bed," he said tiredly.

"No, Carson. Wait."

Katie caught her brother by the arm. "I'm sorry. I was just so worried about you. And I—I have some good news."

"What? Did you find a pot of gold at the end of the rainbow?"

"You could say that. I did get caught in a storm earlier."

His interest was piqued. "I know. I was flying in it."

"Come into the office, Carson. I have something to show you."

She'd taken off Cat's ruined red dress and pulled on a robe. Then she'd put the money in a pillowcase and dropped it in the clothes dryer. When the bills were dry, she ironed out the wrinkles. By the time Carson returned, she'd counted the money and divided it into stacks of a thousand dollars. Her winnings almost covered the top of the desk.

Carson took one look at the bills on the desk and his eyes widened. "What—how? You won?" He couldn't conceal his disbelief.

"I won."

"I don't like that, Katherine. Those casinos are no

place for a woman like you. Promise me you won't do it again."

"I hope I don't have to." Katie counted the stacks. "Eighteen thousand dollars. Is it enough to redeem your IOUs?"

"No."

He'd lied to her. That didn't surprise her, but the amount did. "How much more do you need?"

"At least another ten thousand," Carson said sheepishly. "But with this, I can make a start at clearing up a big chunk of my debts and buy some time for the rest. Thank you, but don't do it again. I'll start first thing tomorrow."

Katie looked at her brother for a long moment. Did she dare let him return the money to Montana? What other choice did she have? She didn't think she could face him again.

"Carson, if I hand over this money to you, will you promise not to gamble with it? Can I trust you to pay off your debts?"

"I'll pay them off, Katie," he said, holding a pile of the money and riffling it through the air. "I promise."

"You've promised before, Carson," she reminded him.

"I know and I'm sorry I've been such a failure. I won't let you down this time, sis. Cross my heart and hope to die."

"All right. I'm going to put the money in the safe. Tomorrow morning"—she glanced at the big clock over the mantel and changed her wording—"make that later today, I want you to take this money to Mr. Montana and settle up. Don't tell him where you got it. And Carson, bring the IOUs back to me."

He watched her gather up the money, studying her with those great dark eyes that always made her want to put her arms around him and promise that everything would be all right. She knew her caretaker attitude to Carson didn't help. But she'd promised their mother and father that she'd look after her brother and she refused to admit that Carson wasn't the honorable man a Carithers was supposed to be.

Maybe this would force him to take hold of his life and be strong enough to find a new direction. Strong, like the man she'd gambled with. The man who held Carson's future and Carithers' Chance in his hands. Hands that had held her earlier tonight.

Long after Carson had gone up to bed, Katie sat in the office, staring out at the night, at the river that rushed by the levee in the darkness beyond the drive. Once there had been fields of cotton, indigo, and sugarcane. When she was troubled she could stand by the window and see those cotton fields in the sunlight. Once the Caritherses' barges ferried all that cotton down to New Orleans. Once the Caritherses had been a family of planters.

All that was gone now. There'd never be any more cotton. The lands, the barges, the family. Only she and Carson and the house were left. And if she hadn't won tonight, Montana would be claiming half of the house.

Carson had assured her he'd redeem his IOUs, but she wasn't certain she could trust him. And the eighteen thousand wasn't enough. She'd either have to face Montana and claim his boat, or she'd have to go gambling again.

Could she return to the *Scarlet Lady*? If she could win again, she'd just give him back his boat. What would she do with a gambling boat anyway? Her father would have called her line of reasoning weak, but after almost losing Carithers' Chance, she couldn't bring herself to take someone else's livelihood, not without trying every other way first. Lady Luck had been with her once. Could she count on winning a second time?

An even bigger question was could she face Rhett Butler Montana one more time? Another kiss like the last one and she might not be able to run away.

Still, if that's what it took to save her family's land, she'd go with Carson in the morning. They'd be a team, protecting each other. This time she'd forget the red dress and the feathers.

She picked up her glasses and slid them on. This time she'd face Montana as the woman she really was, an accountant on a mission, a woman intent on outwitting a gambler who thought he had the power to take everything she held dear.

FOUR

After Carson went to bed, Katie took a shower, washed the river water from her tangled hair, dried it, and went to bed.

But she soon found she was too tense to sleep. She'd always had trouble sleeping. Carson slept like a baby, carefree and deeply. At least he used to as a child. His room was on the other side of the house and he came and went at such odd hours, she was never sure anymore.

Her thoughts kept going back to Montana. The *Scarlet Lady* with its red bed loomed in her mind. What was she going to do? Taking his boat would solve all her problems, but could she bring herself to do the same thing to him that he'd done to Carson? Could she destroy his livelihood?

Part of her said it was business. Gambling was his business and wagering his boat was his choice.

The other part said she couldn't do it. Even if she

had won, she'd misled him. He thought she was just some inexperienced woman, coming in to gamble. He didn't know about her peculiar ability to remember cards, to win at poker. She'd heard that people like her were banned from casinos; their pictures circulated so they could be identified before the house lost a lot of money.

She could understand that. But this time she hadn't used her special ability in her game with Montana. They'd only played one hand. The cards had just come her way. She'd won honestly. She knew that, but a tiny little voice in her head kept saying, "Are you sure?"

Sleep didn't come.

She hoped that sleep didn't come to Rhett Butler Montana either. Anyone who earned his living preying on the weaknesses of others should have trouble sleeping. Still, in all fairness, everyone who gambled wasn't weak. To some, it was just fun. And a man could throw his money away any way he wanted, provided he could afford it. The men who ran the casinos ought not be held accountable for those who were addicted to gambling.

Katie realized that her judgment was skewed. Another peculiarity in her character was trying to see both sides of a problem. She ought to be concentrating on Carson instead of rationalizing Rhett Butler Montana's lifestyle. But every time she closed her eyes, all she could feel were the gambler's dark eyes, his overwhelming presence. Worse, in the darkness the breathless feeling that had filled her when he'd kissed her returned.

Damn the man!

All that was important was that she'd won, faced down the devil in black and won. She'd known he was dangerous; Carson had claimed he lulled you into betting more than you could afford. Even Cat had tried to discourage her from going there to gamble. But until she'd seen the man for herself, she hadn't understood the power of his appeal.

A smooth talker, she'd expected. But the kiss had been a shock, and the aftereffects of that kiss still lingered. She'd been kissed before, but never like that, never a kiss that jarred her so badly that she couldn't trust her own judgment. That's why she'd run away. She'd come face-to-face with her own weakness.

And she'd escaped short of—of what? Being talked into playing another hand where she would lose everything? Of willingly spending the night in that red bed that seemed as much a part of Montana's personality as his clothes?

Discovering that her winnings came to eighteen thousand dollars had been a surprise. Learning that they weren't enough to redeem Carson's IOUs was a disappointment. They needed ten thousand dollars more. How had her brother let this happen? She'd known he was in trouble. Why hadn't she been able to stop him?

Because the precedent had been set by their father. When she'd been younger she'd fought for a place in the family business. She'd even studied accounting so she'd have the right background. But her traditional father had been adamant. Carson was to inherit the company. Katie would have enough money to support her for life and the plantation would belong to the children jointly.

To keep peace in the family and to honor her father's wishes, she'd backed down. She'd convinced herself that shipping goods up and down the Mississippi didn't interest her as much as her work as director of finance at Sacred Heart Hospital. Through her efforts and her family connections, they'd set up an annual Halloween charity fund-raiser at Carithers' Chance. That one event was about to get the hospital out of debt and they were attracting good doctors once more. That was important to the people along the river. And the credit was given to the Caritherses.

But Katie knew now that she should have insisted Carson let her help in the business. She wouldn't make that mistake twice. It might be too late to save Carithers Shipping, but once the plantation was out of danger, she'd have to do something about Carson's problem— "addiction" she finally said out loud. And that would take more money. In the wee hours of the morning she reached a decision, the only decision. There was no other. She'd go out gambling again. If she could win enough to clear their debts without claiming Montana's boat, she'd do it.

But she'd do it somewhere else.

She'd barely managed to escape Montana's magnetism tonight. A second encounter could be fatal. Next time she might not get away unscathed. In the morning, she'd accompany Carson to the *Scarlet Lady*, but she'd avoid Montana by waiting in the car. With her close by, Carson wouldn't dare gamble.

The sun was already turning the night sky from black to a mottled gray when sheer exhaustion overtook her and she finally closed her eyes. It was almost lunchtime when Katie woke and discovered that for the first time in a very long time, Mary Katherine Carithers had overslept.

And that Carson and the money were gone.

She dressed quickly and dashed downstairs and around the house to the garage. Carson's car was gone.

And so was hers.

Calling Cat proved useless. She wasn't home, or if she was, she wasn't answering. Katie grew angrier by the moment. If everything she'd been through went for nothing, she was going to disown her brother. Yes, she'd always been his champion, but enough was enough. At the rate he was going, Carithers' Chance would be changed into a casino and they'd be reduced to living on a houseboat on the river.

On a normal Sunday, she'd go to church, then on to the hospital finance office, where she'd put in a few hours of work. Today, she was stuck at the house. Of course, she could call Montana and tell him . . .

Tell him what? Don't let my brother gamble the money I won from you? Suppose Carson hadn't gone on board Montana's boat? Suppose he'd gone somewhere else? No one was going to listen to her pleas. Gambling was their business and Carson had money.

Unless . . . She went to the phone and called the police.

"Police department. What is the nature of your emergency?"

"My brother is missing."

"Your name please." The operator went on as if she'd said the same words a thousand times.

Katie gave her name and address and that of her brother.

"Oh, yes. Carson Carithers," she repeated. "And how long has he been missing?"

Since—since this morning."

"I'm sorry, ma'am. Mr. Carithers is an adult and he's only been gone a few hours. Unless you have reason to suspect foul play, we can't file a report for twenty-four hours. Please call us back if he doesn't turn up."

With that the operator hung up. Katie let out a breath of despair. She would never get the police's help. Not in time. Lunchtime came and went.

Katie paced. Finally, swallowing her pride, she dialed the office of the *Scarlet Lady*. "Mr. Montana, please?"

"He's out of the office for the afternoon," the receptionist said. "May I take a message?"

She declined. If Montana was gone, nothing could be done about Carson anyway. She had to believe that he'd made good on his promise to turn his life around. Katie brewed some iced tea and wandered out onto the veranda. But all the empty flower urns brought back memories of begonias and roses and the other blossoms her mother had once grown in such profusion. But that was before. Before her parents had been killed in that fateful plane crash over the Okefenokee. Before the last of the Carithers fortune began its steady downward spiral.

Mid-afternoon came.

Still no Carson. What was taking him so long? When he finally got back, she intended to give him a tongue-lashing for not calling. No, not a tongue-lashing, an out-and-out screaming fit of anger was what she'd give him. From now on there would be no more excusing Carson for his carelessness. He was almost thirty years old. "I'm sorry" and a hangdog look wouldn't be acceptable anymore.

When she heard the sound of a car drive up to the house and stop, Katie dashed toward the front door and flung it open. "Where have you been?"

The man standing on the porch was a gambler, but he wasn't Carson Carithers. Even wearing faded jeans and a New Orleans Saints T-shirt, Rhett Butler Montana was still formidable. But this time he was as startled as Katie.

"You," she said in disbelief.

He leaned against the door frame and studied her, then let his lips curve into an amused smile. "Well, well. So Katherine Carithers is the lady in red."

"Where's my brother?"

"Your brother?"

"Yes, my brother, Carson. He went to see you this morning."

"I haven't seen your brother, Katherine."

"I don't believe you."

"Believe me. I haven't seen him for over a week. I can honestly say that if I never see another member of the Carithers family, it will be all right with me."

Katie was beginning to have a very bad feeling in the

pit of her stomach. She was also beginning to believe the man, something she couldn't allow herself to do.

"Don't lie to me," she said in a low, desperate voice. "The money in the safe is gone."

The catch in her voice was almost imperceptible, but Montana heard it. In spite of her calm facade, he knew she was bordering on hysteria. He'd had enough angry encounters with women to know how to deal with them calmly, but something about Katherine Carithers had set him off last night and facing her in the daylight didn't lessen the impact.

But having his honesty questioned was one thing he didn't tolerate. His reputation for being straight with his customers was legendary. And he expected the same in return.

"Where is he?" she demanded. "I sent him to pay you. He left here with eighteen thousand dollars. He was to pick up his IOUs and bring them back to me."

Montana gave a disbelieving laugh. "Let me see if I have this straight. You gave your brother, a gambler, the eighteen thousand dollars you won from me? My money was to pay off the IOUs I hold. What kind of thinking is that?"

"What do you mean, *your* money? I won it—fair and square."

There was nothing light about his laugh then, or uncertain. "I don't think so," he said. "I still haven't figured out how you managed to cheat at blackjack, but I know how you won at poker."

Katie gritted her teeth. It was worry over Carson that made her bristle, that kept her from discussing the problem in her normal logical way of handling a crisis. "You're accusing me of cheating? I don't have to listen to this."

"Oh, but you do, darling. I'm on to you. And while we're putting everything on the table, I think you'll agree that under the circumstances, you can forget about claiming my boat. It stays right where it is. And I'm willing to forget filing charges if you return the cash."

"Filing charges?" She'd had a royal flush. Her hole card had been the queen. She'd beaten Montana and she wouldn't be treated like some criminal. Of course, it was likely her hasty exit made him question her. She wanted to lash out at him, tell him it had been his bed and his touch that sent her swimming in the darkness. If he hadn't kissed her, she wouldn't have bolted. But he had and she did.

And that's why he was here. Somehow he'd found out who she was and he'd come here to weasel out of the bet with some trumped-up charges.

"What do you mean, filing charges? I won. I won the bet and your boat. You're just trying to get out of paying off. Is that what you did to Carson when you enticed him to put up the house as a wager?"

Was that possible? she wondered. Could he have somehow goaded her brother into making foolish bets as Carson had said? Well, she'd gotten even. She'd won Montana's boat and a lot of his money. If she hadn't panicked and run, Carson would have had more than enough money to settle his debts. Then something else occurred to her. If she won, the pot was to have been doubled. Montana owed her more money *and* the *Scarlet Lady*.

Rhett Butler Montana didn't deserve her charity. He'd come here to threaten her. So much for having a good conscience. She'd just take his casino and sell it. That should wipe the slate of debts clean and leave a nice chunk of change for repairs around the plantation. All she had to do was force this bandit to pay off.

Collecting a gambling debt wasn't the kind of credit and collecting she normally dealt with, but the same procedure ought to work as well on IOUs as it did on corporate accounts.

Katie pushed up the sleeves of her sweatshirt and gave her outlaw adversary a predatory smile. "Do come in, Mr. Montana. And let's talk about paying off gambling debts. About you paying off—double or nothing as I recall."

That stopped him cold. He swallowed his retort, reminding himself that he was here because of Mac. Mac, not the lady in red, nor the fact that she'd cheated and run out on him. She—the woman he was honor bound to help—was also the woman whose dishonesty might have cost him everything he owned. The woman who was accusing him of doing something to her brother. The woman who'd kept him awake most of the night.

She led him through the foyer and into an office that must have been a showplace once. But faded squares on the wallpaper were clear evidence that the furnishings were being sold, probably to pay off debts.

The Caritherses were in deep financial trouble and he'd been sent here to help bail them out, and he had to convince her to let him do so. He had the feeling that she was too proud to accept the help of an outsider, particularly one she didn't know. This had to be between the two of them. For Montana, it was a matter of pride and punishment. Still, he'd been beaten by a woman gambler who cheated and he had no intention of letting her off the hook so easily. She thought he was here about the bet, he'd just let her think that for now.

"I'm here," he finally admitted, "to get my money back."

That statement stopped her cold. "I'm sorry. What did you say?"

"I said, you cheated me out of eighteen grand and my boat."

"You didn't have to play poker with me. It was your choice."

"It wasn't my choice to play with a marked deck. I run a straight game. My word is my bond. I expect the same of the people I gamble with."

"A marked deck? I don't know anything about a marked deck."

"And when people lie to me, I see that they get what they deserve. And you, my pretty lady, aren't going to get away with cheating me."

"Are you threatening me?" she asked, incredulity making her voice thready.

"Believe me, Miss Carithers, I don't threaten lightly. I have the deck of cards that prove you cheated."

She walked around behind the desk and sank into the chair behind it. "That can't be. I don't believe you.

How could the cards be marked? They were new, still in the wrapper."

"There are ways. Where did you get them?" Montana asked softly.

"Why, I got them out of Carson's . . ."

Her voice trailed off. Surely Carson hadn't played with marked cards. If he had, he should have won. But Carson was so bad with numbers that even marked cards might not have helped. She looked down at her hands and saw she was holding the arms of the chair so tightly that her fingers were turning white.

Montana watched as she forced herself to let go and lean back. She closed her eyes as if she thought he might go away if she couldn't see him.

Montana took a deep breath. Getting her hackles up wasn't going to solve the problem. He wasn't just here for himself. He'd given Mac his word he'd help. He had to find a way to calm things down. "No, Katie, in spite of what you may think, I'm trying to help you."

"How did you find me?"

"I have my ways, Ms. Carithers. Trust me. I know what's going on along the river."

Katie shuddered. No matter what he said, there was no mistaking Montana's threat. He really was one of the bad guys and she was beginning to think she hadn't gotten out of Dodge. As much as she wanted it to be otherwise, she believed him when he said Carson hadn't repaid the money.

"I don't know how to convince you, Mr. Montana, but I can't worry about what you think right now. If you haven't seen Carson, I have to find him."

Montana didn't know where young Carson was, but if he was to be found, he and the lady in red had to work together. If she refused to work with him, he had to make her see that she had no choice.

That shouldn't be too difficult. She was totally different this morning, almost as if she were another person. The faded gray sweatshirt she was wearing looked like one of her brother's castoffs. It was too big, covering that luscious body, which she'd been so quick to show off last night, like a tent. The jeans were faded and worn, fitting her legs like a second skin. There were no feathers in her dark hair today, only a headband stuck on with little thought to style. In fact, she looked more like some street waif than the shady lady she'd been in the casino. Some tough street kid.

"If your brother used marked cards, I would have known it," Montana said. "Any other time I would have known you were playing with a marked deck, but last night I was distracted."

"You'll have to prove the cards were marked."

"I have a witness, and I have the cards and the wrapping with your fingerprints on them locked in my safe. So if you don't want me to go to the authorities, you need to listen to what I have to say."

Katie stared at him, eyes wide. "I know you have reason to distrust me, but I'm telling you that I always win at poker. I have this crazy mind that can keep track of cards and probabilities."

"I don't trust you, Katherine, but it wouldn't matter anyway. We only played one hand and you were the dealer."

"And I think you ought to remember that the money I won playing blackjack was with your cards and you were dealing. I won fair and square and you can't prove any different."

Montana walked over to the desk and placed his hands palms down on it, leaning over her. He wanted to jerk her from behind the desk and shake her. She believed what she said was the truth, but he didn't believe it for a moment. She cheated.

"Listen, you little witch, you're in way over your head here. You don't deserve it, but I'm going to find your brother so don't give me any more BS."

She leaned forward in the faded leather chair. "I don't think so, Mr. Montana. I don't need your help and I don't believe a word you've told me. I think it's time for you to go now. I'm going to call the police."

"Excellent idea," he agreed. "Because if your brother is running around with my money, I want him found before he loses all of it."

"He isn't gambling." She came to her feet, laying her hands on the desk palms down, the tips touching his. "Carson wouldn't do that. He promised."

"And this is the first time he's promised?"

"No," she admitted reluctantly. "But this time I'm sure he learned his lesson. He doesn't want either of us to go out gambling anymore."

"Don't worry. You won't be allowed to."

She'd almost reached the end of her control. She had to make Mr. Rhett Butler Montana go so that she could decide what to do. "What you want is unimportant."

"What I want is very important," he said.

Everything she said was being overruled by a man who seemed intent on taking over her life. She lashed out desperately. "Well, it looks like I won't have to gamble anymore. Not since I own a boat."

Montana sucked in a breath, pressing his lips together as if he were trying to restrain himself. Clearly, he was about to erupt. Slowly, he sat down, took a cheroot from his pocket, and unwrapped it.

"I don't allow smoking in my house," she said.

"I'm not smoking," he responded, jabbing the thin dark cigar in his mouth. "I'm thinking."

"About what?"

"Be quiet, Katie. I'm going to tell you a story that not many people know."

"Sorry, I don't have time to listen to fairy tales. If you really haven't seen Carson, then I have to find him. And quick. He may be in trouble."

"I'm fairly certain he is. And I really think you'd better call the police."

She couldn't hold back a hollow laugh. "The truth is, I already have. I'm afraid they know Carson too well. When they're talking about a Carithers, they pretend they're concerned, but they don't do anything."

"That's what I thought. So, it's up to me."

"Not you, Mr. Montana. Me. I'm the only family Carson has left and I'll take care of the problem."

"Why should you? Why not make him responsible for his own mess?"

She looked at him as if he'd lost his mind. "You don't understand about family. My brother is all I have left, and while I may not approve of his actions, I'll never turn my back on him. It just isn't the way I was brought up."

"And I suppose you tote that barge and lift that bale," he said with a humorless laugh. "What I'm wondering about is how you're going to like the landing-in-jail part. I don't think Carson will be around to get you out."

"Carson will be there if I need him," she protested. "Obviously you don't have family, Mr. Montana."

"Not anymore. At least not according to them."

"They probably disowned you. I can understand that." She'd flung out that accusation without thinking. From the look on his face, she knew she'd unwittingly found the truth.

"I'm sorry. I didn't mean . . . I mean I'm certain they . . ."

"You're right. They disowned me. When I was seventeen I did something they said they could never forgive. They haven't. I wasn't as fortunate as your brother. I didn't have a sister to bail me out. I had to find my own way."

Something about the pain in his voice stopped her anger.

She couldn't imagine what kind of family turned their back on a seventeen-year-old, no matter what he did. "And you did it," she said softly, "all by yourself."

"No," he said, standing. "I was as wild as your brother—for a while. Then someone helped me. If not for a stranger, a man I didn't even know, I'd probably be dead or in jail—like your brother is going to be."

She came around the desk, grabbing both his upper arms in a death grip. "Dead? Do you know something about Carson you're not telling me?"

"No, not yet. But I will. If I have to find him to get the two of you off my back, that's what I'll do. What time did he leave here?"

"I'm not sure. I . . . I overslept. It was almost lunchtime when I got up and he was already gone."

"Well I was on board the *Lady* and he didn't come there. I would have been told."

"Where could he have gone?"

Montana let out a deep sigh and disentangled himself from her grasp. "God only knows. With that much money in his pocket, he could be in Vegas by now."

"No, he wouldn't—" Katie began.

"Katherine, he would. The sooner you accept that, the better off we'll both be."

"We? Thanks, but I already told you, Carson's my problem. I'll handle him."

"No, Carson's my problem now. And if I'm going to find him, I'd better get going."

"I'm going with you."

"Until I know where he is, you aren't going to get involved. There are some people who aren't as kind to cheaters as I am."

"If Carson had cheated, he wouldn't have lost."

"No, he would have been caught. I caught you and my guess is that you're better at it than he is."

Katie swore. The man was like a bulldog tugging on the south end of a grizzly going north. "One last time, I don't cheat."

"One last time. The cards will prove that you do."

"Hmph! I can see we're not going to get anywhere."

"Not as long as we argue. I'll call you and let you know if I find him." He started toward the door.

"I won't stay here. My father ruled my mother's life, and to a degree, Carson's and mine. Because I loved him and I thought he knew what was the right thing to do, I let him. But I was wrong." She looked at Montana. "I'm not about to let you do that. I'm going with you. And you can't stop me."

She had a point about control. She wasn't the first one to accuse him of taking over. But from the look on her face, Katherine Carithers wasn't about to let that happen here.

Montana replaced the cheroot in his pocket, shrugged, and started toward the door. "Suit yourself."

Seconds later she slammed the door behind them. "We'll have to take your car. Carson is driving mine."

"He took your car? Why doesn't that surprise me?"

"His car must be in the shop," she fibbed. She might want to string her brother up by his thumbs and torture him, but that was a family matter. "Let's go. Vegas is a long drive."

"Aren't you going to lock the house?"

"Nope. There's not much left inside to steal. If anybody wants to come in, they'll just break a window, and that costs money to repair."

Montana thought about his childhood home along the Battery in South Carolina. Though the house belonged to a stepfather who'd come into his life when he was only a boy, it was the only home he'd ever known.

His stepfather had kept it locked tight, protecting what he owned. The thing he had protected most was his reputation. Until Montana had ruined it.

Now Katie was throwing her reputation to the winds, riding down River Road with a notorious gambler. "Where do we go first?" she asked.

"The possibilities are endless. From Silver City to New Orleans, there must be a dozen gambling boats."

Montana hoped that Carson had chosen one of them instead of the private games that moved from place to place. If he'd gone underground, he'd be harder to find. The only good thing about that kind of game was its high stakes. It wouldn't take him long to lose his money. Except, those people didn't fool around. There were no IOUs. It was pay up or toes up.

Montana had made it a practice to avoid those people.

Now the lady in red had thrust him right in the midst of the biggest gamble of his life. He figured that no matter the outcome, he'd lose either way.

He glanced over at Katie, at her lower lip caught between her teeth, and her dark hair flying in the wind. She was one determined lady. Nothing was going to stop her from saving her family—or her land.

Though he didn't believe a search would find Carson, he knew nothing else would satisfy Katie. So, for the rest of the afternoon they searched for Carson Carithers. Nobody had seen him. Or if they had, they weren't admitting it.

Montana didn't mention Katie's cardplaying again, but he made it a point to keep her away from the tables.

And Katie didn't mention Montana's charge that she'd cheated. Instead, as if they'd agreed on some unacknowledged truce, they talked of normal, everyday things.

They stopped for a late dinner at a small restaurant just off the interstate. Montana chose an outside table, overlooking the bayou.

"What would you like?" he asked.

"I don't care." Katie was weary and heartsick. Nobody had admitted to seeing Carson. "Just something light."

He ordered pasta with shrimp and, remembering her choice of drink at the casino, iced tea. "Tell me about Carithers' Chance."

Katie's eyes lit up. "Of course I never saw it at its best, but it covered over a thousand acres at one time. Before my father's time, the Caritherses grew cotton, indigo, and eventually sugarcane."

"Your father didn't do any planting?"

"No. By then, most of the land had been sold. The last two generations of Caritherses concentrated on the shipping business."

"And the house itself? I'll bet it was once a showplace. Why haven't you opened it to the public like some of the others?"

"My father never wanted that. Other than the hospital fund-raiser at Halloween, he didn't welcome visitors."

"Fund-raiser?"

"Oh, it's a very grand occasion. The house is decorated by the Ladies of the Heart, an organization that raises money for the hospital. We offer a costumed din-ner-dance and a full range of gambling, all for charity, of course. Surely you've heard of our Mississippi Mad-ness Charity Ball."

"Yes I've heard of it, but I've never been invited. Not on the right social register, I guess."

Montana saw Katie's stricken look. To ease the awk-wardness of the situation, he turned the conversation in another direction. "Where did you go to college?"

"It was a small college you probably never heard of—Weldon—close enough that I could live at home."

That figured. "And Carson?"

"LSU, of course. That's where Daddy went."

"And he belonged to a fraternity?"

"Sure. All the Caritherses pledge Sigma Alpha Epsi-lon."

Montana nodded. He knew the scenario. "And you?"

She shook her head. "Me? No. Mother wanted me to go to LSU and become a Tri Delt, but I . . . I didn't."

Montana didn't have to be told that she didn't do either because the money went to Carson instead of Ka-tie.

"What about you?" she asked. "What did you do before you became a casino owner?"

He laughed. She hadn't asked if he went to college, so he didn't volunteer that he had, not right after high school, but eventually. He rarely displayed his bachelor of science in agriculture. It didn't fit with his waterfront persona.

"You don't want to know," he said. "Nothing as glamorous as you and your brother."

"Glamor isn't what it's cracked up to be," she admitted. "If you aren't careful, it becomes a fantasy world that shapes your life forever."

"Yeah. But there are other kinds of fantasies. Once, I thought I'd study law. But I'd never be able to represent someone who was guilty."

"Then why law?"

"I guess I thought it would be a quick way to make a name for myself."

Katie took a quick look at Montana. He was serious. "Was that important, making a name for yourself?"

"No. I guess not. My stepfather wouldn't have been impressed if I'd been elected governor. Not that I'd ever be a politician. Though"—he laughed—"being a politician isn't that far removed from being a gambler."

A long-legged white crane swooped across the water and came to a stop on the base of a leafless cypress tree near the deck. He perched silently, as still as the dark water beneath his view.

She hadn't been hungry, but Katie soon found herself relaxed enough to eat. They talked about their mutual love of the river, of Louisiana with its old-world charm and easy pace. It seemed unreal, this ordinary small talk, this revealing of the past and dreams that she never spoke about. And she was certain that Montana didn't volunteer this information easily.

"Did you always want to be a—what is it that you're called?"

"Financial officer," she answered. "Don't laugh. I wanted to grow cotton. I even took Agr classes."

He almost choked on the bit of bread he was eating. Of all the things he might have expected, her interest in agriculture was the last. It was too much of a coincidence. She'd studied agriculture because she wanted to grow things. He'd studied it because he wanted to show his stepfather that he could be a landowner too.

"Why on earth would you choose cotton?"

"I don't know," she said. "Seeing fields of growing things is like a promise. It's something that's always been. It's a connection with the past and the future."

Montana's goals weren't so lofty. He'd just wanted to prove he could make more money than his stepfather. "Were you a philosophy major in school?" he asked.

She laughed lightly. "No, that was Carson's field. I'm much more practical than that."

"But why cotton? Why not sugarcane or a crop less risky. Growing cotton sounds more like something I'd gamble on."

Her eyes lit up as she began to talk about cotton. "They've developed new strains now, disease- and insect-resistant. I believe it's the crop of the future. Just think, we might even be able to bring cotton mills back to this country. I know that sounds odd, me wanting to be a farmer."

Their waiter lit big fat candles in the middle of the table as the moon began to rise over the tree. Its pale reflection rippled in the water. Sometime, when she hadn't noticed, the bird had disappeared. Now night frogs began a chorus in the silence.

He knew about the new strains of cotton. He kept up on farming, even if he'd long ago given up the idea of impressing his family by being a plantation owner. "You'd like to be a farmer," Montana repeated. "No, I don't think that's strange."

He smiled and pulled an imaginary harmonica from his pocket. Pretending to play, he whistled a haunting rendition of "Swanee River." "Katie, you're a throwback, a real Southern woman with the kind of pride that started a war."

"And you, sir"—she laughed—"are the carpetbagger Yankee who's come to collect the mortgage."

With that off-the-cuff quip, her humor vanished. There *was* a mortgage, and Montana, in an odd way, held it. He, more than Carson, could change her life in ways she was only beginning to understand.

"We'd better go," she said, crumpling her napkin and pushing away from the table. "I've kept you away from your business much too long."

"You didn't keep me," he said. "Besides, Royal can take care of anything on the *Lady*."

But everything had changed and Katie wasn't sure she liked that. Being enemies was easy. Finding out that she enjoyed Montana's company wasn't.

They didn't speak on the drive back. Katie was lost in her thoughts, thoughts about Montana's fantasy of becoming a lawyer to please a stepfather who seemed impossible to please.

Later, at the house, she tried again to release Montana from his self-appointed search. "I appreciate what you've done. But really, you don't have to go with me anymore. I'm sure the police will soon find my car. I do thank you for your help, but I'll find my brother."

"Katie." He reached out and took her hand. "I don't do anything I don't want to do. And what I want to do is pick you up after work tomorrow afternoon."

Startling her with his gentleness, he leaned over and kissed her. "Good night, my lady in red."

FIVE

The next afternoon the late-October day was still warm enough for the top to be down on Montana's sleek sports car. Katie didn't mind. Maybe it would clear away some of her confusion. She'd tried to come up with a way to refuse his help. But when he pulled up in front of the hospital, once again she'd gotten in without a protest.

Montana was responsible for her brother's disappearance, but he'd spent all the previous night helping her look for him. He'd driven her, asked questions for her, and brought her home, saying a quick good night at the door. He'd been the perfect gentleman.

Except for the kiss.

She couldn't dwell on that. She wouldn't think about it, or him. Instead, she'd concentrate on the drive, on his car, sleek and powerful, just like the man who owned it. It was expensive and it was red.

"Don't you know any other color?" she asked.

"What do you mean?"

"Red. You seem to have a thing for red."

They came to a stop at a light, and he gave her a long look. "Well, let me see. I recall a certain red dress. Could it be that you're partial to red, too, Katherine?"

"But that wasn't actually my dress," she said. "I mean I borrowed it. My friend thought it would give me an edge."

"It did."

She caught an errant strand of hair that had curled in front of her face and tucked it behind her ear. He was right. The red dress had given her courage. The red bed in his quarters had taken it away. "Where are we going today?"

"We're going to the *Belle*. I understand your brother used up his welcome there before he switched over to my place. They wouldn't take his IOUs."

"But you did. Why?"

Montana thought about that. "It was strictly business," he finally said. "Your brother bragged about Carithers' Chance so much that I thought it was a mansion. When he offered to put up his share of 'the plantation,' I couldn't turn him down."

Katie couldn't hold back a laugh. "I'm assuming you hadn't seen it at that point. We've sold off most of the land, and the house needs more repair than it's worth. I can't think anybody would want that kind of expense unless it was family."

"Actually I had seen it. I'd driven by it many times. The first time I saw it, it reminded me of my . . . well, let's just say I've been thinking about acquiring a real house to live in."

"Well, you can't have Carithers' Chance," she said firmly. "It belongs in the Carithers family and that's where it's going to stay."

Like the Scarlet Lady *is going to stay in mine.* The long light finally changed and he drove through.

"So why are we going to the *Belle*?" Katie asked, trying not to think about the odd sense of yearning she'd heard in his voice as he told her of driving by her home.

"If we're going to look, we might as well cover them all. It's the next one in line. I know the manager and he has an ear to the river. Maybe he's heard something."

He hadn't. Three riverboats later Montana still hadn't found a trace of Carson. It didn't surprise him. If anyone had seen the missing man, Montana would already have known about it. "It's as if he's vanished," he said as he climbed back into the car. "The only thing I've learned is that there is somebody in a gray limo who's been seen in the casinos talking to some of the gamblers."

"What does that have to do with Carson?"

"Nothing, that I'm aware of. It's just that when you're looking for answers, you look for the unexpected."

"You think something bad has happened to my brother, don't you?" Katie was afraid to hear his answer, but she had about reached the end of her endurance.

"If you mean do I think he's been hurt, no. I think he's hiding."

"Where would he hide? Everybody along the river knows Carson."

"Apparently."

"So," she said, allowing a little discouragement to creep into her voice, "where do we go from here?"

Montana pulled the well-chewed cheroot from his pocket and stuck it in his mouth.

"The manager of the last casino said that he heard Carson had a girlfriend who danced in one of the shows on a boat in New Orleans. As soon as I find out which one, we'll talk to her. Maybe she's heard from him."

"That would be a waste of time. Carson wouldn't be dating a showgirl. He has a fiancée. He's engaged to a girl from one of the oldest families in Baton Rouge."

Montana pulled over into the parking lot of a vacant business. He stopped the car and turned toward Katie. "Katherine, I hate to bring this up. But your brother's actions do not suggest that he has much regard for either honor or etiquette. If you're going to help him and yourself, you've got to start seeing him as he is and not as you'd like him to be."

"You're right," Katie admitted, allowing their conversation to become personal, an occurrence that was far too easy. "I know I have a blind spot when it comes to Carson. It's just that since our parents died, I've had six years of feeling like I'm responsible for . . . everything."

"Too bad they didn't feel that way. Leaving Carson at the helm of a sinking ship was asking for disaster. I'm not sure you can even blame him for its going down."

"I don't," she said. "I never did. The business was

already in trouble. I tried to talk to my father, to help. I could see that his prices were too high. He balked at adopting any of the modern sales and routing techniques and his equipment was hopelessly outdated. He refused to change in a world that was changing constantly. Then he was killed."

"And Carson took over. What had he done up to then to qualify him for the job?"

"Nothing. He was just starting to look for a job as a professor of philosophy. He had to give it up to take over the business."

"Why not you? At least you had the right kind of mind and background."

"Yes. I'd studied business and marketing so that I could help. But my father couldn't or wouldn't allow that. Carithers Shipping Company had always been passed on to the oldest son. That's even written into the original will."

"Even if the son wasn't interested?" Montana asked the question, but he already knew the answer. Over a hundred years had passed since the South and its peculiar ideas of family and tradition had been destroyed, but there were still throwbacks. His own mother hadn't been a true Southerner, but once she married one, grits and mint juleps became the trademarks of her newly adopted life.

"Daddy never gave up hope that Carson would come around. When Daddy died, Carson didn't have a choice. He finally gave in and took over. But it was too late. If Daddy was a poor businessman, Carson was worse. He couldn't admit that he was a failure. I didn't blame him.

The business was doomed. But nothing I could say or do made any difference to Carson."

"Is the business a total loss?"

"It might as well be. The court appointed a bankruptcy attorney to oversee the selling of the company's assets to satisfy our debts. It's just a matter of time."

"You don't suppose Carson used your winnings to pay off some of the business debts?"

"I don't know what to think," was her answer. "Anything is possible, though he'd need ten times that amount of money and then some. No, the only thing that can still be salvaged is Carithers' Chance."

"And I hold Carson's IOUs for his portion of that. Looks like I'm about to become part owner of a Mississippi River plantation house."

She gave him a sharp look. "You claim my house and I'll claim your boat."

"Never happen, lady. I've got proof, remember?"

"And I've got pull. I'm a Carithers. You're a gambler."

Montana released the brake and hit the gas. The sports car shot forward out of the parking lot and into the street.

Carson Carithers was no prize, but in spite of her innocence, his sister was just as bad. Still, until he found Carson, he'd table any further discussion of Katie's cheating. As much as he hated a cheater, he had to grudgingly admire Katie for figuring out how to win. Poor Carson was a washout in every way.

It was late when they returned to Carithers' Chance. Once again, there were no lights on announcing the return of Katie's wayward brother. Montana pulled up to the porch, opened the door, and walked around to Katie's side of the car. But she was already out and heading to the steps.

"Thank you for looking for Carson. I have a strong feeling that by the time you get back to your boat tonight, Carson will have been there. If not, when he comes, please tell him that I'm . . . I'm waiting for him."

"He hasn't been there or I'd know. I have a car phone, or hadn't you noticed?"

"No, I hadn't." She hadn't noticed much except the driver. Katie looked down at her hands. She was still wearing the fake nails Cat had glued over her own short ones. Their bright red color was almost black in the shadows—black like the empty place in her chest. The day had been a waste. She hadn't found Carson, and her emotions had been wrung out to a tight thread that threatened to break at any minute.

"I'm sorry, Mr. Montana. You've just spent an awful lot of time helping someone who must seem ungrateful. I'm not. It's just that—that nothing like this has happened before. Carson has always lived his own life, but he's never done anything illegal, or intentionally unkind."

Montana could have argued. Everything he'd heard about Carson seemed an exercise in "me first." But Katie was very near complete emotional collapse, and nothing would be accomplished by reminding her that it had been Carson's gambling that had brought them to this place.

Instead, he reached out, placing his hand on her shoulder in a gesture of comfort. She was determined to see her brother with a heart filled with love, and for one brief moment he wished that he had a sister who'd cared that much for him.

Then she raised her eyes, misty with pain and confusion. He knew then that he didn't want Katie Carithers as a sister. He wanted her as a woman. Beneath his fingertips, he felt her begin to shiver. Her breath came short and fast and she swayed.

"I'm sorry," she stammered. "I don't know what's wrong with me."

He caught her just as her knees buckled, lifting her in his arms and holding her to him. "Whoa. I know you're grateful for my help, but falling at my feet isn't necessary."

"I feel a little shaky," she said. "If you'll just help me get inside, I'll be all right."

"Sure you will," he agreed, walking up the steps and across the porch. He started to ask for her key, then remembered the door wasn't locked. Inside, he hit the foyer light switch, then hesitated. Parlor or bedroom? he wondered. Then: "When was the last time you had anything to eat?"

"I . . . I don't remember. I've been too worried lately to eat much. Today, I had some iced tea for lunch—I think."

"That's what I thought. Very little sleep, no food, at least one midnight swim down the Mississippi. Where's the kitchen?"

She had slept poorly. And she wasn't hungry, but she

was too tired to argue. Before she could direct him to the kitchen, he'd found it, switched on the light, and deposited her in a rocking chair beside an old-fashioned fireplace. There was a fire already laid, and even though it wasn't that cool, he struck a match to it and watched the kindling flare up. Glancing around, he spotted an afghan on the floor and spread it across her knees.

Quickly examining the kitchen, he discovered the parlor walls weren't the only thing bare. The refrigerator yielded four eggs, some cheese, butter, and milk. In the pantry he found half a loaf of bread and some coffee.

Katie neither directed his actions nor made any comments on what he was doing as he went about preparing an omelet, buttering bread for toast, and measuring coffee into a percolator on the counter. She seemed instead to be half-asleep. Shock, he decided. It was obvious that she'd been overextending herself for some time. Too much work. Too much worry and too little hope did that to a person. From her slim build he surmised that she didn't eat well either.

"A little of Montana's special cooking and you'll be okay," he said, trying, for reasons he didn't understand, to reassure her. She'd already cost him more than he could calculate, but he couldn't seem to focus on anything but the pain in her eyes when she looked up at him.

"I know you don't think so, Katherine, but trust me when I say I understand where Carson is right now. I've been down that road myself, might still be there if it hadn't been for a man who jerked me out of my own state of self-destruction and put me to work on the docks."

He located a skillet and added a chunk of butter to melt.

She turned her head slowly and looked at him as if she were seeing a stranger. "Self-destruction?" she repeated as if his conversation were being received in slow motion.

Montana whipped the eggs in a bowl and added cheese. At least he'd gotten through to her, caught her attention with something he'd said.

"Drifting. Hopelessness. Call it what you like. It was the road to hell, and I was charging down it."

"Why?" she asked. "Why were you self-destructing?"

He set the bowl down and thought about what he would say. Nobody knew the truth about his past. Nobody knew his real name. He'd become Montana through an act of defiance. Cowboys were tough. Men with names like Rhett Butler Stewart weren't.

"You seem so strong. Carson isn't."

"I wasn't always," he finally admitted. He'd already said more about his past than he'd intended to. Talking about himself took her mind off her problems. "There was a time when I was a lot like your brother. I never knew who my father was. My mother wasn't a woman who could live alone. She needed someone to take care of her and she found a man who would. After that, she had a new life. She didn't need me anymore."

"What happened? Did you run away from home?"

"Not then. I was just a kid. It took me five years, but

I found someone who needed me, a gentle soul whose father had provided her with a stepmother who made her as miserable as I was. Her name was Laura. I thought she needed me. I sure as hell needed her. We fell in love. We were . . . getting married. But our families didn't approve. They separated us. I didn't need that kind of family, so I left."

"I'm sorry they hurt you. But families are important, Montana. They give us strength and support. And help us to make wise choices."

He gave a dry laugh. "Wise choices? Like your family?"

She sighed. "You're right. They—we do the best we can. Sometimes that isn't good enough. But family is family and you stick together."

In a voice as cold as ice, Montana said, "Family killed the only good thing in my life. No more family for me."

"But you were only eighteen. Carson thought a lot of women needed him when he was eighteen. I think it was mostly him that did the needing."

Montana didn't know why he continued to reveal so much of himself. Maybe it was because Katie seemed so vulnerable. She needed someone to be close to, someone she could draw strength from. The truth seemed to be more reassuring than his usual surface banter. "Like I said, Carson and I are a lot alike. But I sucked it up and straightened myself out. Look what's happened to Carson."

"Probably the same thing that happened to you," Katie said. "Carson closed himself off from the people who loved him. According to him, life is full of wants, but the only person you can count on to fill yours is you. Unlike Carson, you had someone to help you, some stranger who influenced you."

"I did. And that's what I've been trying to tell you. Now Carson has help, too. He has me."

Katie didn't protest. She didn't understand Montana. His persona and his actions didn't seem to match. She was having a hard time resolving the difference. Montana the gambler seemed different from Montana the man.

She surprised herself with her next question. "What happened to the girl you loved?"

"She died," he said, abruptly turning his back and sloshing the eggs into the hot skillet. Katie might as well know the whole truth. No point in stopping now. "She killed herself. Because of me. And I couldn't stop it because they wouldn't tell me where she was."

Katie found herself standing and walking toward the man she'd sworn to hate. Suddenly he wasn't some evil monster, preying on the weakness of others. He was a man in pain, a man who hurt and needed—just like Carson.

Laying her hand on his arm, she said softly, "I'm sorry, Montana. Death is so final. It doesn't give us a second chance to do things."

For a long moment time seemed to stand still. The only sound in the kitchen was the soft bubbling of the omelet and the burping perk of the coffee. If Montana was breathing, it was so shallow that Katie couldn't detect it.

Then the grandfather clock in the hall chimed, reminding her how late it was and how many nights she'd waited for Carson to come home. Carson was still missing. Carson had to be the focus of her energies now. Realizing how close she'd come to forgiving the gambler who held her future in his hands, she stepped back.

"Your omelet is done," she said. "I'll get the plates."

The spell was broken. The sooner she got Montana out of her kitchen, the sooner she could focus on her responsibilities. Depending on him to find Carson was giving him a strange power over her. She didn't like that. She didn't like how she'd felt only minutes before. Carson was *her* brother. She'd find him.

Katie placed two plates and two mugs on the breakfast table overlooking the garden. She brought silverware, napkins, salt, and pepper. Montana halved the omelet, guiding a slice onto each plate. As he poured the coffee Katie removed the pan of toast from the oven and brought the sugar and cream to the table.

They sat down and began to eat in silence. Beyond the bay window, the twilight was streaked with traces of firefly-studded darkness, hidden behind the gauzy tufts of moss hanging from the low graceful limbs.

The omelet was rich and fluffy, the coffee strong and hot. To Katie, there was an illusion of warmth. Like the glass covering on a glass globe Christmas snow scene, it held them, magnifying the moment. But illusions weren't real. All it took was a gentle shake and the peaceful scene quickly turned into a storm.

She ate, but her movements were mechanical. She couldn't allow herself to be sidetracked by this constant awareness of Montana. Her brother, her home demanded all her attention.

Montana slowly cleared his plate. He neither looked at her nor spoke. It was as if, by bringing her back to life, he'd given up the spirit of his own.

Finally he said, "You're right. We can't change the past. But we can try to change the present. You may not understand it, but that's what I'm trying to do with your brother."

"I appreciate your efforts," she said, "but I can't ask you to give up any more of your time. I'll contact the police. I'm sure they'll be more cooperative when they find out about the missing money."

"You don't understand, Katherine. It's a matter of personal honor. I have to find Carson."

"You're right. I don't understand."

He stood. "It's too complicated to explain. I'm not sure why protecting your brother is so important to you either, but it is and I'll do what I can to help, even though I believe he's a lost cause. Go to bed. I'll call you."

He started down the hall.

"Montana," she called out softly, then stood and followed him. At the front door she stopped and looked up at him. "This would make sense if you were family. But you're not."

He glared down at her, his stern brows set in a line of determination. But as they stood in the half-dark foyer his expression softened and for a moment she thought he was going to kiss her. He didn't.

She was stunned when she realized that she wanted him to.

Finally, she said, "If it's any consolation to you, I won't take your boat and leave you without either a home or a job. The Carithers family isn't heartless." She didn't mention the double-or-nothing pot.

"Well, thank you, ma'am. It's real generous of you to take pity on a poor river rat."

"You're welcome," she said, not realizing that he was being sarcastic until she noticed a thunderous scowl erase any momentary sign of tenderness from Montana's face. Thunder and a stern reply.

"At least my family was honest enough to disown me. Yours just plays games. Are all the Caritherses gamblers?"

"The men have been and they've had a run of bad luck. Me? I never have, at least not seriously. Until the other night. I guess I'm the first winner in this generation. Aren't I?"

He nodded. She was convincing. If he hadn't known better, he'd believe her claim of innocence. "That's debatable. As least you planned your strategy. You had it all worked out, didn't you? Too bad Carson didn't send you out gambling in the beginning."

"He didn't send me out at all. It was my idea. And you lost."

"That's what you wrote on the mirror. But you left so abruptly that we didn't have a chance to discuss it. Usually a big winner is willing to negotiate a consolation prize. I think you owe me one."

"I'll certainly do whatever I'm expected to do. But

I'm afraid I don't know how to be a professional gambler."

Montana shook his head. "In this case, neither do I." He took her face in his hands. "But this will do."

Katie didn't protest. This time he did kiss her. Deeply, completely, with all the need a man keeps penned up inside him. Then he released her, gave her a wicked smile, and said, "That was no consolation prize, darling. I did all the kissing. You still owe me."

He'd done it again—kissed her. And she'd responded—again. Flustered, she lashed out at him, saying the first thing that came to mind. "The only thing I owe you, Montana, is the money for Carson's IOUs. And if you force me, I'll make a legal claim on your boat. I may not win, but I'll tie you up for so long, you'll be glad to forgive my debt."

He leaned against the door, looked her over carefully, and smiled. "There's something you ought to think about, darling. I go with the boat. If you claim you won the *Scarlet Lady*, you won me, too. Maybe you'd better start deciding what you're going to do with both of us."

"What?"

"And lock this door behind me," he said. "I don't want anybody else moving in before I do."

"He says that *if* I won the boat, I won him, too." Katie flung clothes into a small case as her assistant and best friend, Cat, watched.

"Hmmm. Does that mean by claiming his share of Carithers' Chance, he also wins you?"

Katie zipped the case closed with a vengeance. "Certainly not. People don't belong to people."

"You could have fooled me. Listening to you talk about the Carithers family, I thought you owned each other heart and soul."

"That's different. That's Southern tradition."

"So's gambling. Sounds to me like you and Montana won each other. Some package deal."

"Oh! You sound just like him. Bossy and dictatorial!" Katie picked up her case and marched down the steps to the foyer.

"I'm perfectly happy to take a few days' personal leave and go with you, Katie."

"You don't have any left, Cat, you'll have to take time off without pay."

"Okay, time without pay. You can just gamble an extra hand and share your winnings. Call it expense money."

Katie wanted to refuse, but she needed Cat. She needed her courage and, it occurred to her, she needed her car. "All right. You can go."

"I'm already packed," Cat said. "But I would kinda like to know where we're heading."

"To New Orleans."

"Why my car?" Cat glanced around. "Where is the blue goose anyway?"

Katie threw her bag in the back of Cat's Mustang. "Apparently Carson took it."

"And how've you been getting back and forth to work?"

"Montana insisted on driving me."

Cat's "Hmm" was all interest and questions. "Do we know what happened to Carson's car? Or did he use that as part of his wager, too?"

Katie leaned her head back on the seat and closed her eyes. "I have no idea. For all I know, it could have been repossessed. Let's go to New Orleans, Cat."

"You're the boss. Any specific place we're heading?"

"Carson is supposed to be dating a showgirl on one of the riverboats there. I want to talk to her."

"You think she knows where he is? I thought he had a fiancée."

"He does."

Katie never realized how many gambling boats and dinner cruisers there were along the river. The gambling casinos were open twenty-four hours a day. The dinner cruises provided the live shows and entertainment. But none of them gave out information about their patrons.

Finally, just after lunch, they boarded the *Dixie Queen*, a permanently anchored, gaudy paddleboat that advertised the finest entertainment north of New Orleans and the biggest winners at their gaming tables. A sign on the dock announced they were holding tryouts for their show.

"That's it," she declared. "That's how we'll get some answers."

"What's it?" Cat echoed.

"We'll apply for jobs. Get friendly with the other girls and see what we can find out."

"Katie, we only have the rest of the day. We don't have time to waste applying for jobs. Besides, what makes you think anybody would hire us?"

Katie brushed by her friend and started down the deck. "I didn't say we had to get hired. I just said we'll try out. Besides, I took ten years of dancing and you can belt out a fair tune. Let's go for it."

It didn't take any more convincing to sway Cat. She was always up for something new. However, Katie wasn't nearly as confident as she tried to sound. She had no doubt that Cat could pull it off, but there was no way she could become a chorus girl.

Minutes later a short bald man was walking around them, studying both women as if they were prize steers and he was a butcher. "Tell me again about your experience," he said, glaring sternly at Katie.

"I've had ten years of ballet, tap, jazz."

"So has every girl south of the Mason-Dixon line," he said. "Experience, lady. Where have you worked?"

"Well," she improvised wildly, "I spent some time on the *Scarlet Lady*."

"Montana's boat? I didn't know he had a show."

"He sometimes offers shows," Cat threw in. "For special occasions, for private parties. I was the singer."

With that, she pulled up a stool near the piano, picked up the portable mike, and began to sing. By the time she told Bill Bailey to come home, the man holding the auditions was nodding his head in appreciation.

When the song ended, he walked over, took Cat's hand, and said, "I'll take you, doll. The other one can go."

Cat jerked her hand back. "No way, Jack. We're a team. If she's out, so am I."

"Name's Sam, not Jack. And I don't even know if she can dance," he protested.

"Sure she can. Would a Carithers lie to you."

A stiff, disbelieving look washed over the manager's face. "You related to Carson Carithers?"

"I'm his—"

"Friend," Cat finished. "Friend of a Carithers was what I meant. It's Carson who's the black sheep. He ran off with her car and we're still looking for it. Do you know Carson?"

"Oh, I know him all right."

"Then you've seen him?" Katie asked, losing her stiffness in her eagerness to hear his answer.

"He was in here a couple of nights ago."

Katie let out a deep sigh of relief. He was all right. He hadn't been murdered and thrown overboard by the mob. "Do you know where he went?"

"Nope. Saw him talking with a man in a suit. Then both of them took off."

Cat spoke up. "Can you tell us the man's name?"

"Nope. All I know is that he travels in a gray limo. Comes in here to hassle my customers and never spends any money. If he shows up again tonight, I'm going to have him thrown out."

"Oh." Katie's disappointment was overwhelming. They'd come so close. But he'd said *again tonight*. That meant the man came often. "Do you think he'll be back?"

"Maybe. Maybe not."

"Please," Katie said, "the money's not important. If you'll give me a job, I'll do whatever you ask. It's really important to me. To get my car back, that is."

"Your car—yeah. Look, ladies, nobody ever said Sam couldn't appreciate a woman who's been done wrong. Knowing your friend, he'll probably be back when he finds some more cash. Tell you what, I'll make you a deal. I'll give you a job for a couple of days, and I'll ask around about the guy your boyfriend left with."

Katie looked at Cat. There was no point in correcting his impression that she was a woman wronged. This might be a lead to Carson. She turned back to Sam and nodded. "What do we have to do?"

"The redhead can sing and you—maybe you'd just better start out hustling drinks. We'll play it by ear from there."

"Thank you, Sam," Cat said. "I'm Cat and this is Katie. For tonight, we're yours."

That remark turned out to be a complete error. Even without her Wonderbra and feathers in her hair, the tight red shorts and cutaway had the same effect. The patrons on the *Dixie* thought the waitresses belonged to them, particularly the new ones. At nine, the boat left port, traveled upriver, returning at midnight with no sign of Carson.

By one o'clock, one of the gamblers who struck it big ordered a bottle of champagne. When Katie brought it to his table, he decided that she'd brought him good luck. He'd gambled there for over a year and this was the first time he'd won. There was nothing for it except that they have a drink.

"I'm sorry, sir," she said backing away, searching desperately for Sam. "I'm not allowed to drink while I'm working."

"Oh, I think Sam would approve. He gets enough of my money to keep him happy."

Katie found herself being pulled to a corner table and shoved into the seat. "Please, don't do this."

At that moment Montana, dressed in his work clothes, the black frock coat and string tie, appeared in the hall. He clamped down on his usual unlit cheroot and forced himself to swagger across the room toward Kate, who was trying to back away from the customer.

"Hello, darling," he said. "Are you ready to go?"

"Montana," she said, springing up and moving toward him. "I'm so glad to see you."

"And I'm glad to see you," he said, pulling her close and planting a kiss on her forehead. "Who's your friend?"

"Oh, he's a lucky customer. He just won the jackpot."

"Congratulations, buddy. But I think you'd better find someone else to celebrate with. Let's go, sweetheart."

He turned and, pulling her into the curve of his arm, started toward the door.

"What are you doing here?" Katie asked in an angry whisper, resisting his attempt to get her out the door.

"I came to keep you out of trouble. Looks like I'm just in time."

"Okay, so you rescued me. Now let me go!"

He had a grip of iron. "Not yet, darling."

"How'd you know where I was?"

"Sam called. Wanted a reference on you. When he said you performed for me at private parties, I couldn't resist accepting his invitation to be at the one he was arranging for later tonight. I didn't think you'd start without me."

"What do you mean, a private party later tonight?"

"That's what I thought," he said. "Don't you know what entertaining at private parties implies?"

She gasped. "But we just meant singing and dancing."

"We?"

"My friend Cat and I. I'm the waitress. She's a singer."

Montana groaned. "Where is she now?"

"She went on upstairs to the party. I'm supposed to be bringing up a special bottle of whiskey after I served that man back there."

Montana glanced around the room, catching sight of a red-haired woman just as she exited the elevator and marched toward the door. "Katie, we're not going to find out anything," the redhead said. "We're getting out of here. We just quit."

"Can you swim?" Montana asked, remembering the last time Katie left in a hurry.

"No," Cat answered. "Do I have to?"

"Not this time," Montana said, putting an arm

around each woman. "We're back at the docks. I'm Montana. Let's get out of here."

"So you're the bad guy?" Cat said, looking up at him. "I'm Cat. You didn't tell me he was a man to die for, Katie."

"He's not."

"No, I'm worse. I'm the private party Katie's entertaining later tonight."

SIX

"Just how far were you two planning to go to get *my* money back?"

Montana drove Katie to Carithers' Chance with Cat following in her own car.

"The money wasn't our objective. We were trying to find Carson. Sam said he was in his casino Sunday night, talking with a man with a gray limousine but nobody knows who he is. We thought if we went to work for Sam, we might learn something."

"Did you?"

"No," was Katie's answer.

"Well, I did. The man's name is Leon. The scuttlebutt is that he's some kind of vampire who appears in the night and disappears before the sun comes up."

"Vampire? Come on. That's ridiculous."

"I agree. I'm only repeating the talk along the river."

"So what does Leon have to do with Carson?"

"I'm still working on that."

Katie loosened her seat belt and leaned forward. "Can't we go and talk to him?"

"Good idea," Montana agreed. "Know where he lives?"

"No," Katie admitted with a frown.

"And neither does anyone else, so far as I can tell."

"But the police," Katie suggested. "Surely they can find him."

"The police are looking for him too. It seems several people have disappeared after being seen talking with our mystery man."

Katie gasped. "You mean he kidnaps them?"

Montana shook his head. "No, I don't think he kidnaps them. Think about it, who'd want to kidnap a gambler that loses all the time?"

"But there must be someone who can help us find him. Maybe the news—a television reporter?"

Montana looked skeptical. "I can't get anybody to publicly admit that Leon exists. The casino owners don't know, and the gamblers won't talk. If he isn't a vampire, he's a ghost. A reporter will only drive him further underground."

Katie leaned back, making no attempt to cover her disappointment. "So what now?"

"We wait. I put out the word that there is a reward for information about either Leon or Carson. Until somebody comes forward, we'll just have to sit tight."

"What about Carson's girlfriend, the showgirl?"

"She works for Mario, who used to deal for me. But she hasn't seen him either."

"So you found her too."

"No. She found me. She's a very nice girl named Emily, who said that Carson left her, heading for my place to pick up his IOUs. Later he called her. He seemed despondent, told her he was a failure and a screwup. He ruined everything he touched and he wasn't about to hurt her or anybody else anymore."

Katie paled. "You don't think he—"

"No, I don't."

"But you can't be sure he hasn't done something to himself, can you?"

Montana could be reasonably sure. What he didn't tell Katie was that Carson had made several stops between Emily and the *Scarlet Lady*. It hadn't taken him long to lose a good portion of the money he was carrying. But according to witnesses, he still had money at the last table where he'd gambled. Where he'd gone from there, nobody knew. If anything bad had happened to Carson, Montana was certain he hadn't done it to himself.

Laying her head back against the seat Katie closed her eyes. "Of course he hasn't. He's my brother, I'd know if he was . . ."

She couldn't say "dead," but Montana knew what she meant and he couldn't stop himself from reaching out and taking her hand. When she grasped his tightly in return, he felt a protective twinge.

"He's not dead, Katie. He's just missing. I'll bet he'll be home by the time we get back."

At that moment his car phone rang. Releasing Katie's hand, he lifted the receiver. "Yes?"

"Royal here, boss. A man just came by and left a note for you. It might be from that Carithers kid."

"We're on our way. Don't leave the dock until we get there." He hung up the phone and turned to Katie, who was holding her breath. "No, it isn't your brother. But someone brought a note Royal thinks might be from him. I'm going straight to the *Lady*. Okay?"

She nodded.

He pulled over to the side of the road and left the motor running while he went back to inform Cat of their change of destination. "You go on home. I'll see that Katie gets there."

"Okay," she agreed, "but you take care of her. She's got a blind spot you could drive a truck through when it comes to the people she cares about. I wouldn't want to see her hurt."

"If Carson hasn't already accomplished that, nobody ever could," was Montana's reply.

"That's where you're wrong, gambling man. She hasn't figured it out yet, but you could hurt her more than her brother ever has."

"That just might work both ways," he said softly.

Cat let out a sigh of exasperation. "Men. How come Katie always draws the needy ones?"

Needy? Him? Cat was blowing smoke. If there was one thing Montana wasn't, it was needy. He'd learned to do without family and commitment completely. There'd been darn few women who'd done more than pass through his life, and his only friends were his employees. The last thing he needed was a woman who filled her heart and life with needy people.

The last thing he needed was Katie Carithers.

Why then was he climbing back into his car and taking her hand? He was reassuring her, that's why. It had nothing to do with the fact that it reassured him as well.

He didn't need reassuring. He needed a steak, a drink, and a woman.

Any woman would do.

From the look in Montana's eyes when she climbed out of the car, she realized the skimpy black cutaway and red satin shorts that passed as a waitress uniform were more revealing than Cat's cocktail dress.

"If you ever decide to give up bookkeeping and take up bartending, you'd make a fortune in tips," Montana drawled.

He took her arm and supported her as they walked up the ramp onto the boat. As soon as they were inside, she felt a lurch as the doors closed and the boat moved away from the dock.

"No," she protested, turning back. "We can't leave until we've read the note. Suppose we have to go somewhere?"

"We'll just go back," he said, gathering her closer as they made their way through the din of noise from the slot machines and the people playing roulette. They took the elevator to the third level, quiet by comparison as the more serious players concentrated on their cards.

Royal met them halfway across the floor. He handed the envelope to Montana, though his eyes were drawn to Katie and her costume.

"Don't ask," Montana instructed, pushing past Royal, ignoring his smirk as he led Katie down a narrow corridor that led to an entrance to his private quarters.

Inside, he flicked on the light switch, bringing the lamps beside the bed to life, then led Katie to the red couch and dropped down beside her.

"What if it isn't from Carson?" she asked through clenched teeth.

He ripped open the envelope and pulled out the folded slip of paper and the bills it surrounded. "It is. He says he's sorry, but this is all that's left. He's going away for a while and I should tell you that he's very sorry for the trouble he's caused."

Every nerve ending in her body seemed to collapse. She felt numb, as if she'd been submerged in a cold mountain stream, immobilizing her so that she could barely speak. "How much is left?"

Montana counted out the bills. "Eight thousand dollars exactly."

"Oh no! He lost ten thousand dollars of the money I won. How could he do that?"

The money you cheated to win, Montana wanted to say. "For him, I'm afraid it wasn't hard. Whoever taught him to play cards ought to be shot."

She wasn't going to cry. Instead she felt as if she were splintering before him, ready to snap as her teeth chattered lightly.

"It was me," she said. "Can you believe it? I taught him one Christmas when I was in college. We had a cabin in Colorado where we'd planned to ski, but there were avalanche warnings, so we played cards. Carson wasn't very good at it. He always lost, unless I let him win. I never dreamed he'd do this. It's all my fault."

"Don't freak out on me," he said, taking her hands in his and rubbing them briskly. "It isn't the end of the world. After all," he quipped, "he doesn't need to be good. With your special talents, you can win that back and more in one night."

"You don't understand," she whispered. "It isn't the gambling. He's never gone away before. If there was trouble, we'd face it together. Like family."

Montana didn't want to argue with her loyalty. He found it honorable, though foolish. Nobody had ever stuck by him like this. If they had, they'd have helped him find Laura. Quickly he shut off that kind of regret. It was destructive. Carson had one thing right; the only person a man could depend on was himself.

If Carson had faced the trouble at the company in the first place, Katie might have managed to steer him in a direction that would have kept it from going under. She wasn't blind about anything except her brother. From what he'd learned, and he'd made it a point to find out, Katie Carithers was a bright, hardworking woman who'd done wonders at the hospital. Why were the Carithers men too blind to see what she could have brought to the table?

One lone tear trickled down her face. She wiped it away.

"Don't worry, Katie," he heard himself saying. "I'll find him." He put his arms around her and pulled her close. "I promise."

Commitment. The thing he'd just said he'd managed

to do without. He'd jumped into it with both feet. Giving Mac his word that he'd straighten out this situation was a matter of honor. Promising Katie was something else. He just wasn't quite sure what.

"Thank you," she whispered, and leaned against him. She didn't move, allowing him to hold her, to comfort her. Finally, she asked, "But where would he go? He has no money. Apparently he has no car."

"Think about it for a moment, Katie. He didn't gamble away all the money. He stopped. That has to mean something, doesn't it?"

She became still for a moment. "Yes. I guess it does."

"And he's never done that before, has he?"

"No. I don't think so."

"Then, for tonight, I think we have to give him the benefit of the doubt.

"I suppose you're right. It's just that I've done that for so long. I guess I'm tired. Will you take me home?"

"Darling, Katie. I can't."

"Why not?"

"We're on the river, remember? In an emergency I would turn the boat around, but not otherwise."

His fingertips gently massaged the tension-tightened muscles in the back of her neck while his other hand clasped her to him.

"But—"

"Just relax, Katie. My guess is that you haven't slept any better than I have since we met."

"You've had trouble?"

"Yes. I've had trouble. It isn't every day that a

woman comes on board and"—*cheats me out of my boat and my money*—"and jumps over the side," he finished.

She smiled. "I suppose not. I'll bet you have to throw most of them off. I don't know why you're helping me. Not after . . . after what happened."

Because I gave my word to Mac, he could have answered. But that wasn't the full truth. He hadn't even called Mac to give him a report. "I'm not sure I can explain," he finally said. "For now, let's just say I'm offering you a place to rest for a while."

"I can't. I have to keep looking for Carson."

"For once, let someone look after you," he whispered, stroking the curve of her cheek and her neck as if she were a small child who needed reassurance. "Just pretend I'm a member of your family and stop worrying. I've left word all along the river. If Carson turns up, anywhere, I'll be notified."

Neither of them said anything for a long moment. Katie knew she ought to push him away, but she couldn't force herself to move. She'd never felt so protected, so safe, and it scared her.

Little by little she melted against him, relaxing until he was supporting her completely.

"Why? Why are you really doing this?" she asked again.

Sliding his hands beneath her legs, he lifted her into his lap. She tensed for a moment—

"It's all right," he whispered, taking her hand in his and holding it loosely.

—then relaxed again as the smooth rhythm of his heartbeat against her ear reassured her.

"I don't understand," she murmured.

"Don't try. I think, just for tonight, you need a friend, someone who isn't asking for anything in return. Let me take care of you, Katie. I won't harm you, I promise. Trust me."

She didn't know how to answer, so she didn't. She was just too emotionally exhausted. For once, she'd let someone else take charge. She just sat, encircled in his arms, feeling his strength and allowing a strange sense of calm to settle over her.

"I'm going to put you in bed now, Katie, just to let you rest. Nothing more."

She heard his words, but didn't feel threatened. Warmth spread through her body, relaxing her even more. His movement only added to her feelings of safety, safety that was abruptly threatened when he laid her down and started to move away.

"No," she cried, her voice sounding husky and strange in her ears. "Don't." She looped her arms around his neck and pulled him back. "Don't leave me."

Montana groaned. All kinds of alarms were going off in his head, alarms and misgivings and pangs of responsibility that he didn't want to feel for this woman who had crashed into his life and left it reeling in the wake of his obligation to Mac. She was a cheater who would go to any length to protect what was hers. She was even willing to forgive the brother whose wrongdoing would be the final act of destruction against one of the oldest families in Louisiana. He didn't understand that kind of family loyalty. But he couldn't dismiss a grudging respect for the woman he was holding.

Respect and something more.

Desire. Not just sexual desire, but a deep, desperate longing to have someone feel that kind of loyalty to him.

She made a small soft sound and pressed herself closer.

"You don't know what you're asking, Katherine Carithers," he said, smelling the sweet jasmine scent of her hair, feeling the subtle movements of her body against his.

"I just want to be close to someone," she said, a kind of muted desperation evident in her voice. "Just for a while. Please hold me, Montana. Tonight I want . . . I want to forget about everything."

"All right," he finally said. "Let go of me, just for a moment while I take off your shoes."

She allowed her arms to slide limply to the bed. Montana stood. He pulled off her shoes and eyed the waitress costume skeptically. The long-sleeved cutaway was twisted around her.

"Let's take off this jacket," he said, and waited for her to object.

She didn't. Instead she let him lift her and slide the coat off her shoulders, leaving her with only the glittery tube top and the satin shorts. When she unzipped the shorts and lifted her bottom, a shocked Montana peeled the slinky garment away, revealing a pair of lace panties that didn't begin to conceal the dark silky hair beneath.

He groaned.

Until now she'd kept her eyes closed. They opened and Montana caught his breath. Her eyes were smoky, glazed almost with what he recognized as need. Sexual? He didn't know. But they beseeched, speaking without words. And he couldn't refuse.

Moments later he flicked off the lights, removed his frock coat, his tie and boots, then lay down beside her. She moved toward him, nestling her head on his shoulder, pressing her lithe frame against him. They lay for a long time without moving or speaking. He listened to the sound of her breathing, felt the familiar movement of the boat in the water, and reveled in the knowledge that in spite of what had happened, she trusted him.

He didn't know how much time passed. She was asleep, or so he thought, when she nestled her fingertips at his nape and said softly, "Montana, do you find me desirable as a woman?"

His pulse went into double overtime. "Yes, Katherine, I find you very desirable."

"Men don't, usually."

"The men you know must be blind, deaf, and dumb."

"No, they just see the woman I am. Your lady in red was a figment of Cat's imagination."

"You can't change a person into someone who isn't there to begin with," he said, trying desperately to keep his body from announcing how much he desired her.

Katie stirred restlessly, her fingertips moving back and forth across his chest, ranging lower and lower.

"I wouldn't do that if I were you. You're lying here, in my bed with almost nothing on. That makes you vulnerable. You're playing with fire, my lady in red."

She gave a nervous little laugh. "You know this bed is what sent me overboard the night we gambled."

He started. "This bed? Funny, when I was trying to figure out why you bolted, I never considered that."

"It was there behind you, all red and obvious. Then I saw all those condoms in your drawer and I—I panicked. Do you make love to a lot of women here?"

"Contrary to what you may think, Katie, I've made love to damned few women here. It's more a matter of being prepared for a situation before you get in trouble. I learned that a long time ago."

One by one, she unfastened the buttons of his shirt, her fingertips dancing across his skin like a skittish colt trying to make up his mind to accept a carrot. With one finger she drew a line across his breastbone and down to one hard nipple. "You're talking about her, aren't you, the girl who died?"

"Yes."

"Did you love her?"

His simple yes said it all.

"And she loved you?"

"She said so."

"So what happened?"

He waited a long time, then surprised himself by answering. "We were just lonely kids and we found a way to make that loneliness go away."

"What happened?"

"She got pregnant. They sent her away."

"And you?" Katie continued to play her fingertips across his chest.

"Me? I went crazy. Almost killed her father."

"Did you look for her?"

"Yes. But I never found her."

"And then she . . . died?" Katie asked.

"Yes. But I didn't know it for a long time. Nobody bothered to tell me. That's when I knew I didn't want to belong to that kind of family. I left and I never went back."

"What about your mother?"

"It was too late. I would only have hurt her."

Katie laid her check on his chest, snuggling into the curve of his arm. "I'm sorry," she said. "Losing someone you loved must have been hard."

"That's a surprising reaction. Considering your background, I would have thought you'd tell me we were too young to be in love. That I was foolish to think a high society girl like that could ever be in love with an outsider like me."

He wouldn't have revealed so much, but talking was the only way he could keep himself from rolling over and taking what she was so innocently offering.

"Why do you call yourself an outsider?"

"I was. My mother was from West Virginia originally. She always wanted to be a Southern belle, but her family was dirt-poor. I never knew my father. When she got pregnant with me, she ran away to Atlanta and went to work for my stepfather's firm. When she caught my stepfather's eye, she got smart. Marriage or nothing. He married her and took her to Charleston. She would have loved Carithers' Chance."

"So how did that make you an outsider?"

"Even now, Charleston is another world. If your

family doesn't go all the way back to the original land grants, you'll never belong." He laughed. "Though she married my stepfather, who adopted me and gave me his name, Stewart, that didn't make either one of us belong. In fact, I tried every way I could *not* to belong. Anything that made a family name more important than the person wasn't something I wanted."

This time it was Katie who felt the pain Montana had bottled up inside him. He was a victim of family, just as she was. The difference was that he'd turned his back on his and she'd taken on the weight of hers. In the end, the result was the same; they were imprisoned by their pasts. And each was alone.

She ought to get up and leave. She ought to be concerned about her brother instead of the man who could be responsible for his disappearance. Lifting her cheek from Montana's chest, she studied his face in the darkness. As her eyes became accustomed to the shadows she could see that he was frowning, tension making lines like a caricature meant to show stern determination. She understood that kind of tension, she'd felt it so often herself and tried to contain it.

Her heart started to pound. Katie turned away, lying on her back, and instantly regretted the distance she'd put between them. "Don't you ever wish your life had been different?"

"Wishing doesn't make it so," he replied gruffly. "It's just an exercise in regret. And regret is destructive."

"And how do you deal with regret?"

"I try not to put myself in that situation. If I want

something, I go after it. I may be sorry I got it, but I'll never be sorry I didn't try."

Katie thought about that. There had been so many regrets in her life, many of them because she'd allowed herself to be turned away from what she truly wanted. And what she wanted now was this man. "Montana, will you kiss me?"

"For Christ's sake, Katie, what are you asking? You're playing with fire."

"I don't mean a passionate, run-for-the-hills invasion. I mean just a sharing, 'I understand' kind of kiss. Please?"

He was going to regret it. But he couldn't refuse. Slowly, he turned on his side, lifted himself to one elbow, and looked down at her. The darkness added a dreamlike surrealism to the room, almost as if it weren't really happening. "This isn't smart, you know."

"Probably not. But maybe I'd like to do something that isn't smart. Maybe I'm tired of being careful. Maybe, for once, I'd like to be a little wild and crazy."

"I'm not sure I know what an 'I understand' kind of kiss is." He lowered his face until their lips were only a breath apart.

"Improvise," she whispered, reaching up, and pulled him down.

Their lips touched, lightly. He only meant to linger for a second, then pull away. But that was before he touched her and felt the shattering of his control. Eagerly she returned his kiss, parting her lips, using her tongue to draw quick little swirls on the inner lining of his mouth.

She moved herself snugly beneath him as her finger-tips danced up and down his back. It was as if she'd been freed, as if the cork had been removed from a bottle of champagne, allowing it to explode.

Montana tried to draw back, but she was having no part of that, and this time it was he who shifted his body so that he could touch her the way she was touching him. He still wasn't certain what an "I understand" kind of kiss was, but he knew that even if their thinking processes weren't in complete agreement, their bodies were.

He moved away. Their gazes locked, the air between them crackling with desire. She was so beautiful. He couldn't hold back a smile.

"Don't smile at me like that, Montana."

"Why?"

"Because it's different. It's a real smile, not a pose. I don't want to think of you as real."

"Are you saying you can deal with whatever this is between us as long as you see me as some smooth-talking devil who seduces the innocent bystander?"

"Yes."

Then slowly, with both of them aware of what he was asking, he lowered his mouth again. No matter how they justified it, the feel of her in his arms was so right. As he leaned in to touch her mouth with his, he saw a flash of uncertainty for a second in her eyes; it disappeared as their lips came together and he deepened the kiss.

A new intensity awoke inside him. He burned with the unexpected need not just to be inside her, but to make love to her. He sought the smooth silk of her neck, her shoulders, sliding his hand lower, shoving the tube top down so that he could reach the small firm breasts that pressed against his palm, exploring, claiming her with his touch.

He slid his knee between her thighs, nudging that part of her that responded and invited entrance. Montana wanted her with an urgency he might have found unsettling if he'd allowed himself to admit it. Instead he felt her turn to liquid beneath him, asking, offering, giving back touch for touch as she pushed his shirt from his shoulders. Then it was gone and she'd pulled away, planting kisses down his chest and back to his face.

On the verge of losing control, Montana rolled away and stood. "Are you sure about this, Katie?"

There was only a brief hesitation. "Yes."

Then slowly, Montana unzipped his trousers, peeling them and his briefs down his legs as he framed what he was about to say. "This probably isn't the smartest thing I've ever done," he said. "I want you like I've never wanted a woman since"—he swallowed Laura's name and said—"I was a kid. But I won't go any further unless you tell me. I said you needed rest, and if you tell me, I'll put my clothes back on and leave right now."

Leave? Katie felt a sudden breath of cold air. No matter how hard she'd tried to hold them close, people had been leaving her all her life. First her father, who turned his back on her offer to help him in the business, then an accident took both him and her mother, and finally Carson's disappearance. She was in dangerous territory here, but she'd been pushed as far as she would go.

Just once she'd stand firm. Just once, she'd get what she wanted. This was a man who wasn't refusing her, who wanted her, who was ready to take what she had to give.

"I want you, too, Rhett Butler Montana."

"Maybe we'd better talk about it," he hedged.

"No talk. No conditions. No tomorrow. Just tonight, my gambling man." She held out her arms.

She heard him as he opened the drawer to the table by the bed and withdrew the protection he promised. She swallowed a moment of panic as, moments later, he lay back down, pulling her gently into his arms. He touched her, tracing the curve of her shoulder, across her neck, and over the top of her breasts. In the time it took for her to take a deep breath, he'd rekindled the low flame smoldering just beneath the surface, turning it into a raging wildfire.

Someone was moaning. She thought it was herself, but it might have been him. He bent his head, taking her nipple into his mouth, pulling on it, nuzzling it, then moving to the other. Every place he touched burned, sending out uncontrollable nerve spasms to her lower body. He slid his leg over her and she could feel him hard and pulsating as he nestled between her legs and rubbed himself against her.

"Montana," she whispered urgently. "Please!"

Then he was inside her, his fingertips digging into her hips, lifting her as he plunged into her again and again. Over and over they rocked against each other, fell away, and met once more. Then they were both flying, shooting through time and space like a comet, burning white-hot, disintegrating as it fell. Until there was nothing left but the afterglow.

And the perfect sense of togetherness that might never again be so real.

SEVEN

Montana slept for a short time, then lay in the darkness with his arm around Katie. He felt extraordinarily happy, almost euphoric. But this feeling of fulfillment was different. It was more than simply sexual pleasure, it was a kind of contentment that was new.

He could hear the slowing of the paddles as the boat headed toward the shore. The lights of the wharf peeked beneath the door to the deck and through a small cut-glass half circle at the top, creating a kaleidoscope of color across the bed and the woman he held. He'd known she was beautiful and stubborn that first night. He'd known she had a good mind. But beyond that, her loyalty and commitment to her brother stunned him. His stepfather had paid lip service to family and tradition, but what he'd really been concerned about was appearances. It was all surface, and when it came down to a choice between loyalty and reputation, family lost.

Katie really cared. She was a forgiving, loving person.

Even so, she was like two people living in the same body. The forgiving, loving sister and the conniving, relentless gambler with an uncanny ability to win at blackjack and poker. If she couldn't do it honestly, she'd been prepared to cheat. But had she? He was beginning to question his own conclusions. Was he ready to forgive her, to excuse her actions? Looking at her face, innocent in sleep, he still found it hard to believe the marked cards. Even in the worst of his own miserable past, he'd never stooped to dishonesty.

Or had he? His loving Laura had been a secret thing. He'd known that it wouldn't be permitted. Was what he'd done any more honest than what Katie had done?

"Katie." Even as he whispered her name she moved, smiling as if she were dreaming. Having a brother like Carson, she certainly deserved good dreams. But he couldn't see those in her future. If he called in Carson's IOUs, she'd lose her home, or, and he smiled at this thought, at the very least she'd have a new roommate.

Roommate? That idea sent a ripple of pleasure down his backbone. Having a roommate like Katie was a fate Montana could consider. But if he didn't get busy and find Carson, she'd probably challenge him to another hand of poker with the IOUs as the stakes. Seeing how smooth she'd been in their last game, he wasn't sure he wanted to play with her again.

At least not poker.

First he'd find her brother, then he'd force him to work off those IOUs on the boat.

No, giving Carson a job in his casino would be like putting the fox in the henhouse. Carson needed to stay as far away as possible from any kind of game of chance. Besides, he had no intention of calling in Carson's bad debts. He'd rather hold on to the IOUs. Maybe that would act as a deterrent.

But that wouldn't stop Katie. Carson was family. And a family debt was her debt. She'd go out gambling again, if not at his place, somewhere else. His mind went round and round with that thought. If she cheated on another boat, she might get caught. Still, there'd be no stopping her. Unless . . .

It had been staring him in the face from the moment Mac called. Carson's IOUs were the motivation for Katie, and Katie had become Montana's primary concern. If they were satisfied, all this would end. She'd relinquish her claim on the *Lady* and go back to the hospital to do the kind of work she ought to be doing. Of course he'd keep Carson's marker for the plantation for now. He wanted to be a landowner for a little while longer.

He felt the boat touch the dock and the engines die. The laughter of passengers leaving the boat drifted through the night air. He waited until all was quiet. Carefully, he untangled himself from Katie and reluctantly slid out of bed. Quietly, he pulled on a pair of jeans and a T-shirt and poked his feet into his running shoes. Fifteen minutes later he'd retrieved Carson's IOUs from his office safe.

Katie thought he'd encouraged her brother to gamble. He hadn't. But he was about to do the dumbest thing he'd ever done in his adult life. He couldn't even explain to himself why he was doing it. He didn't want to think he was making some kind of grand gesture. Instead, he chose to think of it as helping someone the way Mac had helped him. Except, it was Katie he was helping, not Carson.

With a bold slash of his pen, he marked the vouchers *Paid in Full*, negating over twenty thousand dollars in bad debts while he'd repaid his own debt to Mac. Once done, he headed back to his quarters. Holding his breath so that he wouldn't wake Katie, he carefully opened the door and padded inside. He placed the IOUs on the cover where Katie had to see them, then backed out again.

He'd stopped fighting the way he felt about Katherine Carithers. He'd become her protector, reluctantly, but inevitably. Now he'd become her lover. Never before had the two things merged. Even so, he wasn't fooling himself. As a gambler, he was out of her league socially, if not financially. And that was just as well. His experience with society was bad—all bad—and it was too late to go back home and change things in his life, even if he should ever want to reconcile with his family.

Katie had wanted him for one night. But one night, no matter how magical, wasn't forever. Forever was that elusive thing on which songwriters built great hits, and novelists painfully dismissed as unrealistic dreams. And he wasn't certain how she'd really feel come morning when she realized what she'd done the night before. But he thought she'd probably regret her decision. Montana didn't have to be told that Katie didn't sleep around. Everything about her said she was a one-man woman. Once she found her man, she'd be loyal and trusting— rare qualities in today's woman.

Yes, Katie was special.

Except for her cheating. He kept coming back to that. How could a woman he was beginning to care so much about be a cardsharp? Could he ever trust her? Could he have been wrong?

Then he remembered Carson and knew she'd be whatever was needed to save her brother. If Katie were ever to have a life of her own, Carson's addiction had to end. In order for that to happen, he had to be found.

Montana closed the door to his suite and left the boat, all his logical conclusions intermingled with the fantasy he'd just shared, still swimming around in his head. Someone along the river had to know where Carson Carithers was. Montana just had to find him.

But first he had to call Mac. He glanced at his watch again. It was after two o'clock, just about right to catch Mac. Sliding behind the wheel of his convertible, he picked up his car phone and punched in the number for Shangri-la.

The phone rang once. "Lincoln McAllister."

"Mac, Montana here. I still haven't found Carson Carithers. He seems to have disappeared. Any news on your end?"

"None. And I've run a quiet check on Vegas and Atlantic City."

"Damn. I'm worried."

"What about Miss Carithers? Where's she?"

"Katie? Katie is on the *Scarlet Lady.*"

Mac's "hmm" was followed by, "What do you think, Montana? You think the boy's done something foolish?"

"Too early to tell. The bad news is that he left home with eighteen thousand dollars to redeem his IOUs and went straight to the casino instead."

"And the good news?"

"He quit before he lost it all."

"How do you know that?" Mac asked.

"He sent Katie the rest of the money and a note."

"What kind of note?"

"Typical runaway stuff," Montana said. "Basically said he was sorry, that he was no good and was leaving."

"Keep looking," Mac ordered.

"Any information about a man named Leon who drives a gray limo?" Montana asked.

"No. What's the connection?"

"He's been seen along the river, talking to gamblers, including Carson. Nobody can get a handle on him."

"I'll look into it," was Mac's reply. "And, Montana, Miss Carithers is a working girl. It's time she was in bed, her own bed—alone. Do you understand?"

Montana laughed tightly. "Yes, sir. I'm receiving you loud and clear."

"Unless," Mac added with a chuckle, "you're planning to make an honest woman out of her."

An honest woman? Montana muttered good-bye and hung up the phone. Before he lost all his senses, he'd do some more checking along the river. The sooner he found Carson, the sooner his own life would be back to normal.

❖━━━━━━━━━❖

It was full morning when Katie finally stirred. At first she simply stretched, relishing the quiet luxury of soft sheets and a body that felt completely relaxed. If she could just stay like this, remain in a cocoon of warm nothingness where there were no worries or fears.

Allowing herself to drift, she lay content, absurdly happy with no conscious thought of why. She dozed and woke again, unwilling to open her eyes and destroy the warm afterglow.

Rhett Butler Montana.

His name and image suddenly shattered her peaceful state. She sat straight up, the sheet falling away, exposing her nude body, still flushed with warmth.

She glanced quickly around, reached out, exploring the empty bed and drawing in the musky smell of lovemaking. "Ohhhhh," she moaned. It hadn't been a dream. She was where she feared she was, on the *Scarlet Lady* in Montana's big red-velvet-covered bed.

Alone.

Where was he? Did he always spend most of the night making glorious love to a woman, then vanish the next morning, leaving his lady of the night to dress and slink away without any further encounter?

His disappearance left her furious. Then common sense swept over her. Good. She was glad he was gone. The last thing she wanted was to open her eyes to the sight of Montana's powerful body next to hers, wasn't it? Why then did she feel so . . . so rejected? She stretched out her fingertips, smoothing out the rumpled sheet. It didn't surprise her that Montana was gone. Leaving probably made the next morning less painful for both of them.

When her fingers touched the squares of paper, she didn't know what to think. Refusing to look, she gathered them in by touch, her throat tight and her heart racing. Surely he hadn't . . . The low-down gambler. He'd actually paid her.

How dare he?

Then she opened her eyes and looked at the sheets of paper she was holding, looked and felt her heart stop.

Carson's IOUs.

Marked *Paid in Full*.

Carson *had* paid off his debts. Montana had used her. He'd lied to her. The scoundrel. How dare he lie to her?

Then reality set in. It didn't make sense. Carson hadn't paid off any debts. He didn't have enough money to do that. And she still had the money he hadn't lost gambling, along with a note that he was going away. Beside's, where was Carson's marker for the plantation?

What was Montana up to? There was no point in setting up such an elaborate charade. He couldn't have simply wanted to keep her near, make her depend on him. He was a smooth-talking devil with enough experience that she probably wouldn't have been able to resist him if he'd set his mind into seducing her. Why go to all this trouble? No, the IOUs were marked paid for some other reason.

Then she remembered their original bet. He'd said if she lost he wanted her for the night. She'd said she was worth more than just one night. Her face burned. Her worth—her pay for the evening was in her hand. Not only had her brother's gambling debts been settled, Montana really had paid her off.

If Montana had been there, she would have scratched his eyes out. If thoughts could kill, he'd be a dead man. What did he think she was, some cheap—no make that expensive—hooker sleeping with him as payment for a debt? Her stomach churning, she made a decision.

She wouldn't take this insult lying down. Cursing, she glanced at her watch. She was late for work. As she punched in her office number she hoped that Cat was on time.

"Miss Carithers's office," her friend's voice responded.

"Cat, come and get me."

"Where are you?"

"I'm on the *Scarlet Lady*."

Katie didn't have to see Cat to know she was smiling as she sang out, "And why are you there?"

"Don't ask. Just get over here." Katie slammed down the phone, gathered up her cocktail-waitress costume, and pulled it on. She started out of the door, changed her mind, and moved back to the bathroom mirror, where she scrawled a second message to her absent host.

THE BET WAS DOUBLE OR NOTHING. YOU STILL OWE ME!

Moments later she was charging through the nearly empty casino and onto the dock, Carson's IOUs clutched in her hand.

Montana's sports car wasn't in the space where he'd left it. Good. He was gone. She had a lovely vision of nails, roofing nails, scattered across the asphalt roadway. Elegant long nails piercing the tires on Montana's sports car. The idea of him careening off the highway and into a mosquito-infested swamp was delicious. For good measure, she conjured up a couple of snakes as well. The power of positive thinking had gotten her through some very rough spots in her life. But never before today had she deliberately used it for revenge. What the hell, even if it didn't work, it made her feel better.

"Well, you certainly look bright-eyed and bushy-tailed," Cat commented as Katie got into her car. "Did you have an interesting night?"

"Don't ask."

Cat put her car in reverse. "Too late. I already have."

"Please understand. I don't want to talk about it."

Cat hit the gas pedal and smiled. "When a person starts talking about understanding, they're usually trying to justify an action."

Katie leaned back against the seat and closed her eyes. Cat was right. She couldn't blame Montana. She'd asked for an "I understand" kiss. What she'd really been asking for was a "make everything all right" kiss. No, what she'd wanted was the kiss. All the other was rationalization. She hadn't even been honest about that.

"Don't look so striken, Katie. Once in every lifetime, if she's lucky, a woman meets a man she can't resist, a man worth throwing caution to the winds for and going after. Stop beating yourself up and take a risk. Enjoy your gambler."

Katie let out a frustrated sigh. While Carson was going God only knew where, she was giving herself to the man who pushed him into leaving. Not only was she giving herself, she'd been the instigator. Her body still tingled not from anger, as she'd told herself, but from some physical response that she still couldn't explain. In an odd way, she could accept Cat's supposition. It was inevitable that one day she'd do something totally wild, something totally personal. She wasn't so naive that she couldn't appreciate good—no, make that incredible sex.

If he'd left it there, she could have accepted the night for what it was. But the one thing she'd never accept was being paid off for it.

"You don't understand, Cat."

"Then explain."

"I can't. First I have to get home and change clothes. Forget going home first. Take me to buy a new dress."

Cat couldn't hide her look of surprise. "You're going shopping? Now?"

"Oh, yes. You were right about one thing. A woman on a mission has to catch her victim off guard. Can you turn me into the lady in red again?"

"Katherine, my love, you've always been the lady in red. It just took a man to make you believe it. When are you going to see him again?"

Katie fingered the IOUs in her pocket. "When I've won ten thousand dollars."

There was silence. Gold-and-brown leaves blew off the tree-lined road ahead of their car as it sped along.

Off to their left, beyond the high grass-covered levee, came the slow, labored sound of a barge engine. From the limb of a tree near the road, two ghosts, made from sheets, danced in the morning air, reminding Katie that Halloween was only days away—Halloween and the hospital's charity fund-raiser.

Cat slowed the car and looked at Katie. "You want to explain what all this is about?"

"I don't think so. Just hit the gas pedal, Cat. I'm in a hurry."

"You *want* me to speed?"

"Absolutely."

"What about the hospital? If neither of us shows up, they'll think something dreadful has happened."

"Tell them I'm taking a few days' vacation."

Cat laughed skeptically. "Sure. Then they'll send the paramedics. The last time you took any vacation was when your parents died, and that was only three days. If you're not there, who's going to hold up the corner of Angel Memorial Hospital?"

"For the next few days? You, Cat. You've just been promoted to assistant director of finance."

"And I'm immediately going shopping? Won't that look a little odd?"

"I'm the boss. I'll explain."

The car shot forward. "Yes, ma'am. Does my promotion mean that I get a raise?"

"Depends on how much of my job you do."

"Consider yourself replaced," Cat said enthusiastically. "Now, where do you want to shop?"

"Surprise me," was all Katie said.

The salesclerk looked surprised when Katie marched in, still wearing the satin shorts and cutaway jacket. Katie herself was surprised a half hour later when she left wearing a sassy black miniskirt and a leather jacket adorned with silver studs and fringe.

The shoe store next door produced a pair of shiny black boots with silver toes. But when Cat picked up the black felt Stetson, Katie drew the line.

Their arms full of packages, they headed back to Cat's car. "Where to now, boss?"

"Take me home."

Wisely, Cat didn't ask any more questions. Now that she'd set her course of action, Katie was beginning to feel very shaky. Could she do this? Was she really good enough to duplicate her previous success? Did she even want to?

Then she remembered the IOUs burning a hole in her jacket pocket and knew that she had no choice. She couldn't get past them. When she'd given herself to Montana, she hadn't considered that he might think she was selling her body. In the world she knew, making love meant something. One-night stands had always been beyond her comprehension, as was sex for pay. She'd just done both. Her skin burned as she considered how he'd interpreted her actions.

She shook her head. That kind of concern had to wait. Her reputation was unimportant. She'd worry about it later. For now, she had to clear Carson's name. He might be weak, but he wasn't a bad person. Throwing him into the job of running a company that was already going down was enough to push anybody over the rational edge. If she could square his gambling debts, he could go back to teaching, to a life free of business pressures and family responsibilities.

As for squaring herself with Montana, she didn't know how she'd accomplish that yet. The more she thought about it, the more blame she took for their spending the night together. No matter how he interpreted their lovemaking, it wouldn't have happened if she hadn't let it.

And one thing she did know. Everything had gone too far. If she could play poker and win, she'd forget their bet. She'd never had any intention of claiming his boat—even if it meant losing Carithers' Chance. Still, Montana was a gambler and she had won. Maybe she'd better rethink her position on saving the plantation. Too much pain had come as a result of tradition. Maybe it was time to give it up and move on.

Katie's faithful old Chevy—the blue goose—was now parked in the drive, the keys in the switch. The tank was full of gas, and if she wasn't mistaken, it had been washed.

"Carson?" she called out, rushing into the house. He'd come home.

But there was no one there.

She couldn't decide if he'd even been there.

"What's going on?" Cat asked, entering the house behind her.

"Oh, Cat. Carson's still missing. He didn't pay off

his debts. In fact, he lost almost half of the money I won."

"You didn't tell me you gave him the money. Did you really think he could be trusted?"

Katie sighed. "I know. I believed him when he said he wouldn't gamble. I was wrong. I've been wrong about a lot of things, Cat. But not anymore. Little Miss Innocent is getting a firsthand education in 'me first.'"

"And what is *me* going to do with the new duds?"

"I'm going to make some money. I'm going to pay Carson's debts myself and get Rhett Butler Montana out of my life once and for all."

"Not if he sees you in that outfit," Cat observed.

"He won't. I'm taking my business somewhere else. I've probably been banned from gambling on the *Scarlet Lady*. Mr. Butler seems to think I cheat at cards."

"Do you?"

"No! At least I haven't yet. After tonight? Who knows? The lady in black is on the prowl."

"I don't know about this, Katie. I think you'd better make another plan."

"Go to work, Cat. You have to do the job of the financial director in addition to your own. I'll call you."

Cat hesitated. "Maybe I'd better go with you?"

"You've already taken your vacations through the year two thousand."

"But I'm part of management now," she protested. "Don't I get something more?"

"You don't."

"What do I tell Montana when he comes to pick you

up this afternoon? I assume, since you've been out Carson-hunting every night, that he'll be there."

Katie hadn't thought about that. If she canceled their plans now, he'd be ringing her doorbell. No, she'd just leave things alone. "Tell him that I'm discouraged. I left early to think about things. I'll call him."

"I don't think he's going to like that," Cat observed dryly. "Sure you don't want me to hang out with him?"

Katie made her way up the stairs, her arms still full of packages. "I'm sure. If you don't follow orders, you'll get fired. Go."

Reluctantly, the red-haired woman backed down the foyer and out the door. Only when Katie heard Cat's car drive away did she let out a deep breath and sink down to the steps. Everybody thought she was invincible. But she'd been strong as long as she could. Now she was fully deflated and shaking like a leaf.

She thought about what she was going to do. The only difference between her and Carson was that her gamble had become personal.

Katie forced herself to take a two-hour nap and eat a light lunch. Afterward she showered and dried her hair. Pinning it up like Cat had that first night was impossible, so she settled for curling it to frame her face, letting it touch the top of her shoulders. Bright red lipstick and velvet-black mascara gave her a sensual look that she hoped would accomplish her purpose.

Distraction and defeat.

Because of the touch of autumn in the cool October

air, and the memory of her recent midnight swim, Katie chose the newly opened Casino Louisian, a land-based pavilion, as her destination. The sun was already low in the sky when she left the freeway and followed the signs.

The casino looked like a mirage of pink neon and white lace rising from the river. In the fading daylight, the neon sign rippled and a trio of slot machines shot coins into a sparkling bucket. Katie drove up the tree-lined semicircle, coming to a stop at the pavilion entrance, where two eager young men wearing straw hats and pink suspenders appeared at her side.

The first young man eyed her old car skeptically. The second one opened her car door, took one look, and smiled. "Good afternoon. Welcome to Casino Louisian."

He gave her a ticket for her car and the other led her to the door, ignoring another arrival to watch her walk inside.

Cat had done it again, selected an outfit that had made Katie's first two male contacts fall over themselves to help her. So far, so good. She patted her pocket, checking to make certain the zipper was closed. If she lost the money Carson had returned, it had better be at a gambling table. Studying the lobby signs, she said a small prayer that she'd have an even bigger bulge when she left and headed for the change counter to swap her bills for chips. This time she was playing with ten hundred-dollar bills instead of just two.

The clerk behind the ornate white enclosure handed her a sparkly bucket filled with chips. Blackjack hadn't been her original game of choice, but it had served her well the first time and it would give her time to study her surroundings tonight.

Two hours later she'd won and lost. Still she'd managed to more than double her stake and make her presence known. She left the table and wandered into one of the restaurants offering drinks and a buffet of snacks.

Too nervous to choose something to eat, Katie filled her glass with diet cola and took a seat.

"Wouldn't you like something to eat?" one of the waiters asked. "Compliments of the house?"

"I could use a sandwich, but I don't have enough hands to handle that."

Moments later she'd been served a small plate overflowing with food. Since she couldn't be certain how the evening would go, she worked her way through half the plate. If anybody had asked, she wouldn't have been able to tell them what she'd eaten.

The helpful waiter appeared once more. "May I refill your glass?"

"No thanks," she said. "But I think I'd like to try my hand at some poker. Could you direct me to a high-stakes table, a private one, perhaps?"

He looked at her dubiously. "Ah, maybe you'd rather try some of our regular tables, ma'am. I'd hate for you to lose your—shirt."

Katie smiled sweetly. "Oh, that's all right. My daddy gave me a check for my birthday and told me to spend it any way I want. Since my daddy thinks it's so much fun, I thought I'd find out."

Moments later she was led through the tables and up

a curved stairway to the balcony above. At one of the doors her escort stopped, knocked, and went inside.

There was a large mahogany gaming table in a circle of light. In the shadows beyond, six men looked up. One of them, a giant with long hair caught in a rubber band, stood. "Welcome, ma'am. I'm Big Jonah. I understand you have some birthday money you'd like to share with us. Sit down."

"Who said I was going to lose?" she asked, and slid into a vacant seat.

"I'm Little Willie, ma'am," the player beside her said. Do you have a name?"

She placed her chips in front of her and smiled. "Just call me Red."

"That's obviously not because of the color of your hair," a third player said.

"You're right," she replied with a mysterious smile.

An hour later, when she took the pot, the first man left the game. "I guess we know now why you're called Red."

"Yeah," another player snapped. "I figured that out. It's because you're red-hot."

During a quick break for more food and drinks, Katie found the ladies' room, repaired her makeup, and felt the swell in her pocket. She'd been careful not to be too obvious, but figuring out what the gamblers held had been far easier than she'd expected. It was time to turn up the heat.

She glanced at her watch. Almost midnight. She ought to be tired, but she wasn't. Playing with these men wasn't as nerve-racking as playing with Montana.

Still, her nerves were drawn tight and her pulse was racing. Forcing herself to remain calm, she took her seat. "I've still got most of my birthday money, gentlemen. I'm feeling very lucky. Suppose we change the game and raise our stakes a bit."

The four remaining players glanced at each other and grinned. "Sure," one of the men agreed, "what'll it be? Strip poker?"

"I was thinking more about five-card draw, maybe aces and one-eyed jacks wild."

"That sounds pretty complicated," the dealer said. "Are you sure you know how to play?"

"No," she said, unbuttoning and removing her jacket to reveal the skintight T-shirt beneath. "But I'm a very quick study."

She let them take the first hand. Then settled down to do some serious card playing. By the time an hour had passed, the table was down to three players, with an equal number of chips stacked before each player.

Leaning back, Katie took a deep breath and said the words that had, a week ago, literally changed her life for the second time.

"What about it, gentlemen? Double or nothing?"

EIGHT

Frowning, Montana faced Cat, who was guarding the door to Katie's office like a marine drill sergeant.

"What do you mean, Katherine isn't here?"

"Just what I said. She didn't come in today."

"I've been picking her up every afternoon for almost a week. Why didn't she let me know?"

Cat relaxed her hold on the door frame, looking slightly guilty as she said, "I don't know. I think she's got a hole in her head. If you wanted to pick me up, I'd be here."

Montana wasn't sure he believed Cat. But he took the opportunity to push past her and enter Katie's private office. Unlike the house, her office walls were covered with plaques, certificates, and pictures. Katie with children, Katie with patients, Katie receiving the handshake of some pompous-looking award presenter.

On the desk were more pictures of a personal nature. Two elderly people waved from the deck of a cruise ship, the woman an older version of Katie. A young man, se-rious and scholarly, stared out from behind a desk piled high with books and papers.

And plants. Everywhere there were plants, growing in wild profusion. Along the wall was a table with a cof-feepot and cups. Big fat-cushioned chairs with well-worn fabric were pulled up close, as if they were nuz-zling her battered desk.

The office was Katie and her family, both her par-ents, her brother, and those who made up her everyday world.

"Surely," Montana began, "surely the director of fi-nance gets better furniture than this."

"Oh, she gets it and then she passes it on to some other employee who she thinks needs it more. If it were up to Katie, she'd sit on an apple crate and work on a card table. She's very generous with the people she cares about. Or haven't you noticed?"

"I noticed," he snapped. "But that obviously doesn't include me."

Cat walked around Katie's desk, straightening the papers scattered there. "I think you're wrong. I think she cares a great deal about you. But she isn't going to let herself be distracted by her personal needs. Right now Carson is the only thing she's concerned about."

"I wish he felt the same concern for her."

"So do I. Look, I'm sorry about all this. Carson doesn't mean to be an albatross around Katie's neck. It's just always been that way. She's the caretaker and he was taught to accept it. Really, he isn't a bad person. He's just weaker than Katie."

"So where is she?" Montana asked again.

"I truly don't know."

"You haven't seen her at all?"

"I didn't say that. I picked her up early this morning outside the *Scarlet Lady.*"

"So it *was* you. She disappeared. I wondered where she went."

Cat pursed her lips for a moment, then said, "I probably shouldn't tell you this, but we went shopping."

Montana frowned. He hadn't expected that. "And how many times do you and Katie go shopping in the morning on a workday?"

"Before she met you? Never," Cat admitted. "Katie is a stickler for the rules."

"And you bought . . . ?"

"A new outfit for her."

"Clothes? Not another short red dress, I hope."

"No, it's short, but it's black. And it isn't a dress. It's a skirt and a leather jacket. She also bought a T-shirt and a pair of boots."

That confused Montana. He couldn't picture Katie in a Western outfit. Now that he knew her better, he would never have pictured her in a strapless red dress either. She'd worn that in an attempt to distract her opponent. But she'd ruined it by jumping into the river. Why would she go and buy something else equally bizarre?

Surely she wasn't— He didn't want to think what she might be up to. "Cat, tell me she wasn't going out gambling again."

"I can't tell you anything, Montana. I'm sworn to

secrecy. And I don't break my word. I will tell you that she's used to straightening out matters by herself."

"But this is one time she can't do that."

"I know, and I can tell you that she's pretty discouraged. On top of that, she seems unusually tense. I don't know if it's Carson's disappearance, or you. What do you think?"

"Me? I think Carson is on his own. Someone needs to look for Katie."

"She's where?"

Montana swore into the phone and hit the convertible's brakes, ignoring the car horn and squealing tires behind him.

"Tell me that again," he ordered, certain that he'd misunderstood.

"I said," Royal repeated, "just like you asked, I put out the word that you were looking for Katie. About ten minutes ago a man named Sam called. He said she's in a high-stakes poker game with Big Jonah and Little Willie at the Casino Louisian."

Montana groaned. Not Jonah and Willie. She couldn't have picked tougher gambling companions. "Thanks, Royal. Tell Sam I owe him. How'd he find out?"

"The infamous Leon. You know, the guy in the gray limo you've been looking for. He's at Sam's place. Sam figures he's bagged two birds with one shot. Wants to know what it's worth to you?"

Montana pushed the gas pedal to the floor and the

car shot forward. "I'll call Sam myself." Moments later he was talking to the proprietor of the *Dixie Queen*. "Thanks, Sam. I owe you."

"That you do, old buddy."

"Just name your price, Sam. Whatever you want. Is Leon still there?"

"Yep. But I'm about to throw him out. He's annoying my customers. If he'd bothered the winners, that'd be fine. But he always disappears with my best customers—the losers."

"No. Don't throw him out. Hold on to him till I get there."

"I'll try."

Montana hoped Sam could hold on to Leon, but as badly as he wanted the man, right now Katie was his most pressing problem. Katie might think she was the best poker player on the Mississippi, but she was in over her head. Way over her head. The two men she was matching wits and skills with were the two toughest cardsharps on the river.

Montana thought a minute. "I'm going to try to send someone there to talk to him." He needed someone who was close and could get there quickly. Cat. Montana signed off and dialed her number.

No answer. The message on her machine told him, invitingly, "At the sound of the tone, tell me 'everything.'"

"Since you're not there, I can only hope you're with Katie. If you're not, she's playing poker with two serious gamblers at the Casino Louisian. I'm on my way there now. If you get this message, go to the *Dixie Queen* and see if you can locate a man named Leon. Stick to him like glue till I can catch up. He may know where Carson is."

Montana thought about what he'd just asked and decided that while Cat's daring and ingenuity were called for, he just might have put her in danger—if she got the message—and if she followed his directions. After a moment he called his office and was rewarded by Royal's prompt answer.

"Thank God," Montana said. "You're there."

"I'm here. Why are we thankful?"

"A better question is why are you there? Isn't the boat supposed to be going upriver?"

"It is. But I was told you had an important message and I thought I'd better check it out. It's from Mario, down at the Louisian. He heard you were looking for Leon and wanted you to know he's just left his place."

"Yeah, that's what I called about. I talked to Sam. Leon's there now, on the *Dixie Queen*. I want you to go there and find a woman named Cat."

"Uh-huh, and how will I know her?"

"She's a real looker. Tall, red hair, tight clothes. You can't miss her."

"When I find her, what do I do with her?"

"She's Katie's friend. I just sent her there to look for Leon. I want you to make sure she's safe."

"And where are you going to be?"

"I'm going after Katie."

Thirty minutes later Montana pulled into the parking area of the casino where Katie was playing poker. He brushed past the attendants, stopping at the first table inside.

"The poker game. Big Jonah and Little Willie, where are they?"

"Our games are private."

Montana grabbed the dealer by the throat, jerking him across the table. "My name's Montana. I want to know where they are and I want to know now."

"Hey, man, we don't want any trouble around here. Let me call my boss."

"Never mind. Just tell Mario I'm here." Montana let the dealer go, whirled around, and started up the stairs. The first two private rooms were in use, but the players were strangers. Behind the third door he found Big Jonah, Little Willie, and Katie, each holding five cards. There was a pot full of chips in the center of the table. The two men were looking at Katie, apparently waiting for her to answer the last bet.

At Montana's entrance, all three players looked up: Jonah in surprise, Willie in annoyance, and Katie with a quick flash of desperation.

"Montana," Big Jonah said. "Aren't you a little off course here?"

"Oh, I try to fish all the waters, Jonah. Hello, Katherine," Montana said with a deliberate drawl, groaning silently when he took in the short black skirt and fringed leather jacket. She looked like a honky-tonk girl on a night out, all curves and legs. He felt his throat tighten. At least there was a poker table between her and her companions. There wasn't between her body and his. He wanted to grab her and drag her out of there. "I thought you were going to wait for me."

"Sorry. Got tired of waiting. I decided to celebrate my birthday without you."

He pulled out the chair beside her, eased himself into it, and stuck out his legs, casually crossing his ankles. "Bad girl. Birthdays usually start with a nice dinner and a cake. Then fun and games."

"So it's my day and I'll celebrate any way I choose." She smiled at the other two players. "I wanted to play poker. Don't mind him, guys. He just likes to think of *me* as the dessert. Very expensive dessert. Go home, Montana."

"Nah. Think I'll stay. I can't wait to see you take their money."

Willie laughed. "Never happen. I'm a man who likes sweet things, too. And I'm just about to be able to afford a lot of expensive sugar. Unless you're prepared to back the lady, she's out of money."

Montana cut his eyes toward Katie. "Is he right?"

She winced and nodded. "I'm out of money. It's either fold, or come up with something to use as collateral. I'm trying to decide," she said brightly, "what I want to risk."

Montana didn't like the sound of that. What did she have? Bad question. He didn't want to think what she had, nothing except a seedy plantation and, remembering their bet, herself—neither of which he wanted her to bet. On the other hand, he'd already seen what she could do in a poker game. "Can you take 'em?" he finally asked.

"I think so. Want to see?"

"No. If you say you've got the hand, I believe you."

She raised her eyes, facing him straight on, the memory of the IOUs in her pocket reminding her of his opinion of her. "That's pretty funny. You believe me?"

"Okay, Red, cut the chatter," Jonah interrupted. "What are you going to do?"

"Red?" Montana smiled. "So you've heard about the reputation of the infamous lady gambler in red? That doesn't bother you?"

"Haven't heard about no reputation; she just told us her name was Red. Didn't take long to know she meant red-hot. 'Course, right now it looks like she's just about run out of steam."

Montana pulled a cheroot from his pocket, bit off the end, and stuck it in his mouth. "Guess you really haven't heard. I ought to warn you, one poker player to another, I gambled with her and lost."

Willie looked at Montana with disbelief on his face. "She took you? For how much?"

"You don't have to do this, Montana," Katie said.

"Too much." Montana was tempted to say that she'd won his boat, but he couldn't bring himself to do so, even if it would make Willie and Jonah worry. She'd gotten herself into this fix; she'd have to suffer the consequences. The only problem here was that if Katie was cheating again, Jonah wouldn't take lightly to a marked deck.

"Jonah," Willie said, beginning to look a little concerned, "are you sure about this?"

Jonah glared at Willie. "Cut the small talk, Willie. He's just trying to spook you. What about it, Red? You in?"

Katie glanced down at her cards again. "As you can see, I'm out of chips, guys, will you take my IOU?"

Both men laughed. "IOU? Not in this lifetime," Little Willie answered for both.

"If that's all you're offering, I'll just claim your money now," Big Jonah said.

Katie looked down at her hand. She was holding two pairs, kings and tens. Not the best, but it should be good enough. She ought to bet Montana's boat. It would serve him right. Let him see how it felt to really lose his livelihood. With the winnings in the pot she could pay off Montana and anybody else Carson owed, and have enough left over to repair Carithers' Chance. Then she'd give the boat back to Montana.

Katie chewed on her lower lip. Let them think she was sweating. Damn! She *was* sweating. If she lost, they'd both lose everything. Having Montana so close wasn't helping. She took a deep breath and put him and what they'd shared out of her mind. Logically, if she didn't win, everything was lost anyway. For the first time she could understand how Carson felt. She'd have to gamble that her hand was better than either of theirs.

"If you won't take my IOUs, let me offer you another proposition, guys."

Willie looked at Jonah, then said, "We're listening."

"First, I think I'd better tell you who I really am," she said. "You ever heard of the Carithers family?"

Jonah grinned. "Carson Carithers? Sure. Everybody's heard of him. Most of us have taken some of his money."

"Well, I'm his sister."

That brought an even bigger grin.

"We own a plantation on the Mississippi, Carithers' Chance."

"We know. He bragged about it enough." Little Willie shuffled his feet. "So what does that mean to us?"

"The plantation says I see your bet and I call."

"The plantation?" Willie said. "What do I want with a plantation?"

Montana drew himself up slowly, almost like a cat with a mouse in his sights. He'd studied the cards and the table. So far as he could tell, she wasn't playing with a marked deck. And knowing Willie and Jonah, there was more than a little chance that she could lose.

"Now just a minute, darling. You'd better think about that." He couldn't question her ability—not in front of Jonah and Willie—he'd have to do it another way. "Let's don't get carried away. Just throw in the cards and we'll go dancing."

Katie leaned over and patted Montana's knee. She hadn't expected that. He was worried about her losing Carithers' Chance. He'd obviously chosen to forget that she owned his boat. She glanced at Jonah and Willie. This was no time to argue.

"You don't think I can do it?" she asked.

"No . . . I mean, yeah. Hell, I know how good you

are. It's just I'd rather be partners with you than those two."

"Wait a minute," Jonah said. "I think you'd better explain how you own part of the plantation."

"It was part of a bet her brother lost to me," he explained.

Jonah looked at Montana and smiled. "But it's worth more than he owes or you'd own the whole thing. I think I'll take the bet. I might just like being partners with Montana."

"Hey, what about me?" Willie stood up, claiming his place in the game. "I could win the pot too."

Montana cut his gaze toward Jonah.

"Sit down, Willie," Jonah said. "One of us is about to win a plantation and I think it's me. I'm holding four aces, Red." He spread his cards before her. "Read 'em and weep."

Montana saw the color drain from Katie's face.

"Son-of-a—" Willie swore. "Beats the hell out of my three of a kind."

"Well, Red," Big Jonah said with a big grin. "Guess it don't matter what you're holding, but let's have a look anyway."

"No," Katie said, folding her cards and laying them facedown on the table. "You're right. It doesn't matter now. If you'll call me, I'll make arrangements to meet with my attorney and sign Carithers' Chance over to you. But you'll have to give me a few days. There are some details I have to take care of."

"No hurry, Red," Jonah said. "I trust you. Especially

since I have two witnesses to what you promised. I'll call you."

Katie stood and nodded, then turned and moved slowly, almost regally out the door and down the steps. Montana watched the short black skirt until she was out of hearing range, then said, "Listen, you two, you don't want her plantation. It's falling apart. Before you call Miss Carithers, you call me. I figure we can work out something that will make you happy."

It was Jonah who answered. "Sure, Montana. We're always open to being happy, and to tell you the truth, I'm a gambler, not a farmer."

Montana caught up with Katie outside the casino, where she was handing the parking attendant her ticket. "Wait," he said, "bring my car. I'm driving the lady home. I'll have someone pick hers up tomorrow."

Katie didn't argue. When Montana put his arm around her, she sagged limply against him in shock. The attendant returned with the sports car, and Montana helped her inside. Though he doubted that she was even aware of the cool night air, he raised the top and closed the windows.

They drove rapidly through the darkness. It was too late for recriminations and too early for Montana to come up with alternate suggestions. For now, they were just two people sharing the silence and the emotional letdown.

Instead of stopping as he'd planned, Montana drove past the *Dixie Queen*. It was unlikely that Leon was still there, and for now, once again, Katie was his priority. He hoped that Cat had gotten his message and followed through on Leon and that Royal had found her at the Casino.

They were almost back to Carithers' Chance when the blue lights began to flash behind them.

"Damn!" Montana swore, and pulled over. "Sorry, Katie, looks like I've been caught speeding."

"You and Cat," she said in a dull monotone. "Now I know how Carson felt. Tonight we all lose, don't we?"

"Evening, sir," the officer said, leaning into the open window. "Will you show me your license, please."

Montana fumbled in his back pocket and pulled out his wallet. He handed the officer his license and leaned back, recalling Katie's odd remark.

"Mr. Montana, were you aware that you were driving twenty-one miles over the limit?"

"No, I had my mind on something else."

The officer shone his flashlight into the car, spotlighting Katie. "You all right, ma'am?"

"Yes."

He continued to study Katie for a minute, then nodded. "You're Miss Carithers, aren't you? Did your friend find you?"

Montana took a quick look at Katie. "Her friend?"

"Yes. I stopped another driver for speeding last weekend. A lady. Miss Carithers was a passenger then, too. She was soaking wet. Seems she'd fallen overboard and had to swim to shore. Stopped the lady again tonight. She said she was going to rescue you again. Did you take another swim?"

"Not this time," Katie said, "but I should have."

One speeding ticket and fifteen minutes later, Montana pulled up to Katie's door.

"Don't you ever leave a light on when you're coming home late?"

"No. Electricity costs money." She stared through her side window and gave a humorless laugh. "Not that it matters anymore now. The new owner of Carithers' Chance will have to worry about that."

"Why'd you do it, Katie? You don't legally own it, but you could have bet my boat and gotten out of there without losing your home."

"Like you said, Montana, if I cheated, I didn't win your boat. That means I still owe the debt."

"And like you said, Katie, if you didn't cheat, you won."

She turned toward him. "Are you saying you finally believe that I didn't cheat?"

"I don't know. If you weren't good enough and had to cheat to win the *Scarlet Lady*, you would have cheated and won tonight. There was too much at stake, not to. I'm willing to concede that I might have been wrong."

"You mean about the cards being marked?"

"No, about your needing to mark them. By the way, after you left the table, I looked at your cards. Jonah may have won, but with a pair of kings and a pair of tens, I'd have done the same thing you did."

"Do those two cheat, Montana?"

"If they do, nobody's been able to catch them at it. They're just good, too good. They've been banned from gambling with the house. That's why they rent private rooms to do their cardplaying. You didn't stand a chance from the start."

"I know that now."

He reached over and took her hand. She didn't resist. It was as if she didn't care. "Katie, don't worry about Carithers' Chance. We'll figure out something."

"No. I made the bet. Just like Carson, I gambled and I lost. That's it. Maybe it's for the best. One thing I've learned from all this, things and people aren't the same. My father spent all his life trying to protect the business and the plantation. I thought they were part of our family. They aren't. If I'd seen that sooner, Carson wouldn't be gone. Things don't matter. People do."

Katie pulled her hand free and got out of the car. She opened the front door and flicked on the porch light, then turned back to Montana.

"Thanks for coming after me and for driving me home. I'll get my car tomorrow. Cat will take me." She looked thunderstruck. "Cat! Why was she looking for me tonight?"

Montana felt even more guilty. If he told Katie what he'd done, she'd insist on going after her friend. "She was probably just worried about you. I'll check on her."

"You don't have to do that, Montana. And you don't have to help me look for Carson anymore. I'm sure he'll hear about what happened. Now that everything's gone, he won't feel compelled to gamble to deal with our problems. He can teach. You can go back to your boat and all this will be over."

"What about us?"

"There is no us."

There was no emotion in her voice. She sounded like a character in some kind of old-fashioned zombie movie. She was about to tuck him and the night they'd spent together very neatly into the past and put it away. Montana knew she was right. He ought just to go, but he couldn't leave her. Not like this.

Instead, he pushed open the front door and pulled Katie into his arms. "There is an us," he said. "Just listen to me for a minute, Katie. I never thought I'd say this, but you're right, people matter. You matter. And I'm worried about leaving you tonight."

She let him hold her for a minute, then drew in a deep breath and pushed away. "I don't think I believe you. You walked away from your family, gave up, and never looked back. I let you help me because I was concerned about Carson. I told you once that I'm worth more than what you bet. I was wrong. I'm giving these back."

She reached into her pocket and pulled out Carson's IOUs. She dropped them and watched his face as the slips of paper floated to the floor. "I thought at first that you'd lied to me. That Carson had been there and paid you. But then I realized that couldn't have happened, otherwise he wouldn't have had the eight thousand dollars he sent with the note. Yet you marked them *Paid in Full*. You don't have to lie, was having me in your bed worth that much? I don't think so."

Montana raised his eyes, confusion raging on his face. "You mean you thought I was paying you for—"

"Sex," she said, cutting him off. "I understand and that's okay. I've known from the beginning how you felt about getting close to someone. Actually, I should have paid you. I was the one who asked. So, add your price to my bill. I'll just have to pay you off a little at a time. That, or you can take a lien on the house and work out the details with Big Jonah."

"You don't mean this, Katie. You're just emotionally drained. Whether you believe me or not, I wasn't paying for your body. I'm not sure I understand my actions, I just wanted you to stop gambling. The truth is, I'm just as big a scoundrel as you think. But there's something between us and I know you feel it, too."

"No, I don't. Not anymore." She couldn't accept that. No matter what he said, she couldn't believe him. He'd turned his back on his family. How could she trust him to care about hers?

"But you can't give up your plantation. You've never known a life away from Carithers' Chance. What about growing cotton? What will happen to you?"

She pushed him firmly out the door, gave him a long, sad smile, and said, "I don't know. I'm very tired. I guess I'll think about that tomorrow. Frankly, Montana, right now I don't give a damn."

The door closed, and this time he heard the lock snap into place.

Long after the sound of Montana's car motor had disappeared into the night, Katie stood leaning against the door, dry-eyed and stiff. Everything she'd worked for, everything she'd believed in was gone.

Her parents were dead.

The business was bankrupt.

Carson was missing.

She'd lost Carithers' Chance, and Montana was out of her life. Only her concern for Carson kept her hanging on. Even if he had abandoned her, she would never do that to him.

The only hope she had left was that sooner or later Carson would hear what she'd done. There would no longer be any reason for him to hide. Once he came back, one way or another, they'd get on with their lives.

Even if hers would be empty. For one brief moment she'd held success beyond her wildest dreams in her hands. Montana had been right. In the end, a person had to look after himself. Families weren't always there for you, and even if they were, they might let you down.

Montana. Just the thought of his name brought back the picture of him, dark, brooding, handsome, giving her that wicked smile that dared her to be someone different. She'd shared one night of love with the most wicked man on the river. But it, like everything else in her life, was only temporary. Like all the Caritherses since the original Carson, she'd gambled her future for her past. She'd gambled and lost.

She moved slowly up the stairs and into her bedroom, shedding the boots and Western outfit as she walked. Flinging herself into bed, she lay, wide-eyed and numb. Tomorrow she'd call her attorney. Tomorrow she'd go back to work. Tomorrow she'd have to find a new place for the hospital fund-raiser. And she had to find a place to live.

For the first time there was no comfort in knowing that tomorrow was another day.

NINE

"Sorry, boss," Royal said, "Old Leon was gone before we got there."

Montana swore. "What about Cat?"

"I found her all right. She's with me now. Hold on, she wants to talk to you."

"Hello, Montana. Is Katie okay?"

Montana hesitated. "I'm not sure." Cat was Katie's friend, but he didn't feel comfortable telling her about Katie's bad luck. Instead, he simply said, "The cards were against her tonight. She's pretty discouraged."

"Rats! I was afraid that would happen. She was too distracted."

Like he'd been the first night he'd seen her, Montana thought.

"If we could just find Leon," Cat went on, "that would help." There was a long static-filled minute on the line before she suddenly said, "Wait a minute. I don't know why I didn't think of it sooner. René. René will know."

"Who's René?" Montana asked.

"An old friend. A swamp rat. Runs a place between here and New Orleans. He knows everybody from way back."

"Where can I find him?"

"It won't do you any good to go by yourself. He wouldn't tell you how to get to the road. I know!" Cat's voice was suddenly filled with inspiration. "Take Katie. She knows René. René always did have a soft spot for her."

"Katie? How would she know a swamp rat?"

Cat simply laughed. "I know Katie doesn't travel in René's circles, but there was a time when I did. And I got into as much trouble as Carson. René would call Katie and she'd rescue me about as often as she rescued Carson. Trust me, René will help Katie."

Cat gave Montana directions to René's Place, then hung up. Montana glanced at his watch. It was very late. Katie had seemed so completely drained. He ought to go to René's Place alone and let her rest. He ought to, but he couldn't. Leaving her alone tonight would be a mistake. If Carson was with Leon, she'd want to see him. If he wasn't, she'd never believe it until she'd seen for herself.

He turned the car around and headed back to Carithers' Chance. With all the bad things that had happened to change Katie's life, finding Leon would be something positive he could do for her.

Moments later he was knocking on her door. "Katie! Katie!"

"Go away, Montana." Her response came instantly, as if she hadn't moved since he left.

"Open the door, Katie. We have a lead to Leon."

The door opened. "A lead to Leon? How?"

"Through Cat. Come on."

All Katie's lethargy disappeared. Moments later, still wearing the black skirt and jacket and boots, she was buckled inside Montana's car.

He expected questions. She didn't ask any. Instead, she looked straight ahead, her dark hair whipping in the breeze like a fierce Cajun woman straight out of the bayou. He was beginning to understand that the real Mary Katherine Carithers was a woman of many faces.

"Can't you go any faster?" she finally asked.

"Yes, ma'am," he said. "I don't have to be told twice."

Even following Cat's directions, René's Place was so far off the beaten path that Montana almost missed it. There was no sign. Only the zydeco music blaring from the open windows of a building that looked as if it might slide off into the bayou at any moment told him he was there. He pulled into the graveled parking area and under the limbs of a water oak.

"René's Place," Katie said breathlessly. "Of course. I should have thought of him. He knows everyone along the bayou."

"Katie, I know you're anxious, but before we go inside, we'd better have a plan. From what Cat said, René might not like being questioned by an outsider."

She didn't answer for a moment, then straightened her shoulders and turned to Montana with a smile. "Do you like loud music and Cajun food?"

He didn't quite know how to take her sudden change of mood. "Sure. So long as there's plenty to drink."

"I think René can provide that. Follow me. And don't worry. I'm *not* an outsider."

With a long-legged stride that made Montana's pulse race, Katie led him inside. She went straight to the bar, climbed up on a stool, reached across, and hugged an enormous man with a droopy black mustache. "René. It's been a long time."

"Too long, *ma chérie*. Where you been?"

"Working. Working too hard. This is Montana. We're looking for something hot, something cold to wash it down with, and a little information."

"Sure thing. Find yourself a seat."

As if she were a regular patron, Katie headed toward an empty table in the corner, shedding the jacket and hanging it over one shoulder. Montana followed her, along with the gaze of every man in the house. He wished he'd given her time to change into something less distracting.

She picked a chair and flashed him another pulse-raising smile. "Don't look so fierce," she said. "We're supposed to be here to have fun."

"I didn't hear you." He raised his voice. "The music."

She leaned forward. "I know. It's loud. This place is

like your driving—high-energy. I said, don't look so fierce. You'll worry the natives."

"Sorry," he said, forcing himself to get into the mood. God knew, he'd had enough experience in play-acting. But with Katie, it was becoming harder and harder. "It's just that I never would have pictured you in a place like this."

"People that know me would never have pictured me in your casino either. I'm an accountant. Accountants are serious people. You're a gambler, you're supposed to be the daring one."

"And you think I don't look daring?"

"Look around you, gambling man. Compared to René's other customers, you look like a man who's doing some serious waiting."

Though he was wearing jeans and a blue cotton shirt, Montana thought about what she'd said and nodded. With all the bright colors around the room, he did look serious tonight. They'd reversed their roles. Or maybe they'd just let their secret sides surface.

He thought about the Katie who'd presented such a competent, unruffled front to the world, then, when she'd gotten scared, she'd jumped into the Mississippi and swum to shore. He remembered a woman who faced her desires head-on and asked him to make love to her. Judging a person by the public face he or she wore was always a mistake. He'd learned that playing poker. He studied the dark-haired woman across the table. She was laughing. Instead of composure, there was a hint of rebellion under the control, a hint that suggested secret passion, controlled but ever present.

She leaned forward, touching her lips lightly to his, then pulled back. "So, smile, *chéri*. You're in Cajun country. Let the good times roll."

The music stopped for a moment, then began again, the fiddle screaming, feet stomping, and an accordion joining the fracas. Katie nodded, then turned her attention to the postage-sized dance floor where two couples were dancing. Zydeco music, the music of the Cajuns, the dance of passion.

A shout and a sudden increase in the music made speech impossible for a moment. The waiter appeared with plates of steaming red beans and rice covered with chunks of sausage, crawfish, and pungent red sauce.

"If you don't like it hot, you're in big trouble," Katie called out, filling her mouth with food.

"Oh lady, I like it hot. There's nothing tame about my taste buds."

Katie ate, laughed, and during moments of rare quiet, carried on a running conversation with the people at the other tables.

"Been a long time. Where's your fiery friend Cat?" one of the diners asked.

"Left her behind tonight," Katie answered saucily. "I've been manhunting."

The diner's companion cut her eyes to Montana and said, "Well, if this was the one you were hunting, looks like you found a good one."

"No, this is my—"

"Her fiancé," Montana growled.

"My partner," she corrected. "Tonight I'm looking for a gentleman who drives a big gray car, a limousine."

The man at the next table frowned and glanced across at his drinking buddy. "Why you want an old guy like that, sweet thing?"

"Oh, I don't want him. I just want to ask him about the man I'm after."

"And who'd that be?"

"I've been told," Katie said, "that my brother, Carson, might be with the man in the limo."

"Carson?" René questioned as he refilled their glasses, then dropped down in the chair next to Kate, whispering in her ear, "Your brother's a loser, Katie. Give up on him."

Katie leaned sideways, looped one arm around René's neck, playing with his shaggy mustache with one finger. "Carson may be in trouble, René. I need to find Leon. Please? Do you know him?"

René nodded. "I may know him."

Montana had been holding on to the arms of his chair to keep himself from shoving René away from Katie. "You *may* know him?"

René glared at Montana. "Dance with me, *chérie*, and I'll recollect."

René was big, but he was light on his feet. When he pulled Katie onto the floor, everybody else fell back, leaving the two of them to dance. It didn't take Montana long to see that Sam had missed a good chance not hiring Katie as a showgirl. René's hands pulled her close, twirling and turning her to the rhythm. She laughed and talked, flirting openly with the older man as they danced, driving Montana crazy with jealousy. By

the time the song ended, perspiration was rolling down
Montana's face and Katie was out of breath.

"Whoooeee! All them lessons. You still some
dancer," René said, his arm around her waist. "Why you
stay away so long?"

"I don't know, René. I didn't think so at the time,
but maybe Cat and Carson were my excuse to do a lot of
things I didn't dare do on my own. I've missed you too."

When René left the floor, the musicians took a
break, and for a few minutes the customers could hear
themselves talk.

"About this Leon," René said, leaning close to Katie. "He don't like folks to know what he does. He don't
even use his real name. If he did, you'd know him."

"I would?" Katie said. "Who is he?"

"Louis Gaspard."

Katie almost choked. Everybody in Louisiana knew
Louis Gaspard, at least they knew the first Louis Gaspard. He'd been a pirate. Most people didn't know
about the present-day Louis.

"Leon is Louis Gaspard? Is he still around?"

"Sure he is. He don't leave. Just as peculiar as he was
when your brother Carson ran with his boy." René
looked at Montana as if to explain. "Dario was his son.
Dario was the one who got them all in trouble. He was
the one Cat came here to see."

Katie remembered Cat's infatuation with the secre-
tive Cajun. Dario was older and even wilder than Cat.
There was nothing he wouldn't do, hadn't done, or
wouldn't try. For too many of Carson's early years, he'd

run around with Dario, until Dario dropped out of sight.

"What happened to Dario?"

"Killed, in a fire. Drunk, drugged out of his mind. Almost burned down that old pirate's stronghold. Folks say old Leon's gone squirrelly, closing himself and that mute that drives for him up in that big old house like some kind of monk. They say strange things go on up there."

Montana held his tongue for fear of stopping René's flow of information.

Katie tilted her head, gazing at René with the kind of barely controlled excitement Montana wanted to spark in her. "It's still there? I thought the house burned to the ground," she said.

"He built it back, just like it was when the first Gaspard lived in it. Brought in outsiders to do the work so none of us would know where it was."

"So you can't tell us how to find it?" Montana asked.

"No. Never went there myself. Crossing swords with old Leon is something nobody in his right mind wants to do."

A customer got René's attention, taking him back to the bar. "Well," Katie said, as if she were talking to herself, "I guess we've identified our mysterious Leon."

Montana wasn't certain he believed René's claim that he didn't know where the house was. It was the same kind of brick wall he'd run into over and over, a conspiracy of silence.

"You really know Gaspard?" Montana asked, forcing

himself to concentrate on Leon instead of Katie's flushed face and sparkling eyes.

"I know *of* him. At least I knew Dario. Ten years ago Cat was crazy about him. I'm not sure she ever got over him." She stood up, suddenly serious. "Are you ready to go?"

"Sure," Montana agreed, following her toward the door. At the bar he reached for his wallet and pulled out several bills. René simply took them with a nod.

"Take care of her, Montana. Some say Louis is crazy. People around him have disappeared."

"Some good-bye," Montana observed as they went back to the car. Just what Katie needed to hear. Even Montana felt uneasy.

Still, he knew that telling Katie he'd take it from here wouldn't work. If he didn't keep her with him, she'd go off on her own.

"So, any ideas on how we get to this Louis Gaspard?"

"I don't know," Katie said wearily. What she didn't say was that Cat would know. She'd been to Dario's.

"Tell me what you know about the Gaspards."

"Two hundred years ago Gaspard robbed the original planters, including the Caritherses, of everything the Spanish didn't take. Built himself a hideaway in a place so removed from the world that nobody could find it. Apparently, it still is."

"Yep. Everybody's heard about that Gaspard. It's Leon I'm interested in."

"They've always been thieves. Even Dario. While he and Carson were in college, he got arrested for dealing drugs. Then he disappeared from Louisiana. I was glad to see him go. Carson didn't need his kind of influence. And neither did Cat. Now Dario's dead and Carson . . ."

"Is missing," Montana said.

"Oh, Montana," Katie's voice broke. "Do you think he's all right?"

This time Montana couldn't hold back. He folded his arms around Katie and pulled her close. "Of course he is."

"I hope you're right."

"I am. I'll get you home. Once we find Leon, I'm sure he'll be able to lead us to Carson."

Katie didn't argue. It felt too good to be held. She didn't think either. The feel of Montana's arms around her took her thoughts in a direction she didn't want them to go. For now, she'd just accept this and his comfort.

When they reached the plantation, it seemed natural for Montana to give Katie a good-night kiss. She didn't resist. She knew he wanted her, but he didn't force the issue. Desire burned between them, and sooner or later they'd either smother it or set it free.

The next morning, Katie went into her office early. She needed to rearrange her schedule. Cat was late when she slid in the office side door and headed for her desk.

"And where have you been?" Katie asked.

"Nowhere. Just overslept."

"Oh, then I didn't wake you?"

Cat's eyes widened. "Wake me?"

"I've been trying to call you. You didn't answer. Then your car phone was busy."

"Uh, yes. I was talking."

Katie stood and paced back and forth for a long serious minute before she stopped and walked over to Cat's desk. "Who were you talking to, Cat?"

"I . . . I . . ."

"It was Montana, wasn't it? He called you."

"How did you know?"

"I know how Montana's mind works. Once he learned that you and Dario were lovers, it made sense for him to get to you. What I didn't expect is for you to tell him how to get to Leon before you told me. You did, didn't you?"

"Not exactly. I'm not really sure where the house is."

"But you have been there, haven't you? Otherwise how would you know where it was?"

"Yes. It was the last time I saw Dario. We went to the hideaway. It was a mistake. He was out of control. I didn't mind a little wine, but he got stoned. He scared me. I found my own way home."

"How?"

"By pirogue."

Katie reached over, took a map from her desk, and unfolded it. "Show me."

"You can't go by yourself, Katie. I'm not even sure I could get back there again," Cat said. "I'll only tell you if you go with Montana."

Something in Cat's manner told Katie that was the only way she'd get the information she wanted. "Of course," she said.

"You promise?" Cat narrowed her eyes suspiciously. She wasn't quite sure she ought to believe Katie.

"Why would I lie?" was Katie's firm answer.

Cat hesitated. "I think I'd better come along."

"No, you have to meet with the charity-ball committee in my place. I've already arranged it. They need someone to help with the final plans."

"But it's your ball," Cat protested.

"But Carson is my brother. And I'm still the boss around here."

Katie was studying the map when her phone rang. She toyed with ignoring it, then decided it could be Carson. After the fifth ring she picked it up. "Hello?"

It was Montana. "Are you all right?"

Her heart raced. It was the last voice she wanted to hear, the one voice she couldn't allow herself to respond to. "What do you want?"

"To know that you're okay. You weren't going to answer the phone, were you?"

He knew her too well. "No, I was—um, busy."

"I wish you were here with me."

"Stop talking like that. I don't want you to—"

"Yes, you do. I can hear it in your voice. That's the only time you're honest, when you're not looking at me, when I can't touch you." He'd meant to keep the conversation on a strictly business basis, but once he heard her voice, that became impossible. "What are you wearing this morning, Katie?"

"I'm wearing a skirt and blouse," she snapped.

Montana groaned. "Not that little black one you wore last night?"

"Of course not. I'm at work."

"What color is it?"

"What difference does that make?" she snapped again.

"Tell me?"

Looking down at herself, she groaned. "It's red," she said. And suddenly she was back in his quarters on the *Scarlet Lady*.

She was back in his bed.

Back in his arms.

She could hear him breathing. The heavy silence between them wrapped her in memories, shared memories. She knew that he was there with her, that volumes were spoken by the pictures conjured up by words not said.

"No," she whispered. She wouldn't be influenced by this man. No matter that he seemed bent on coming to her rescue, on protecting her. No matter that he thought she had cheated. No matter that he didn't laugh when she said she wanted to grow cotton.

She couldn't let that confuse the issue. Everything had been said and done. Logically, she couldn't be responsible for Carson any longer and soon there would be no Carithers' Chance. And Rhett Butler Montana was totally wrong for her. But she couldn't stop caring.

"Please," she whispered again. "Don't keep doing this."

"What?"

"Talking like we . . . like we . . ."

"Like we've been lovers? We have. Like we belong together? I'm beginning to think we do. Ah, Katie, you can't hide behind looking after your family forever. And I can't pretend family isn't important. We've been stripped of our defenses. This is between you and me. You may as well stop fighting it. I have."

She didn't know what to say. She couldn't give in to desire. Desire was temporary and she wanted so much more. "I can't," she managed to say. "You and I have nothing in common. You're everything I can't—don't want; a man with no conscience, no roots, and no interest in commitment."

"And you're a woman who's more concerned with the past than the present. You know what they say. Opposites attract. If that's true, we're magnetically connected."

He was right. "The answer to that, Montana, is to avoid each other. Magnets can't attract if they aren't together."

"You can fight it, darling, but in the end it's inevitable. The fates have seen to that. You need me to get to Leon."

"Why?"

"Because we have to go by boat."

She'd been right. Cat had told him. "I don't understand," she stalled, trying to find a way out. "If there's a house in Louisiana, there has to be some kind of road, doesn't there? What about Leon's limo?"

"Don't know about the limo. But the only way I can find to reach the hideaway is by water. Old Louis was a pirate, remember. He sailed."

"And you're a sailor?"

"No, but before I became a gambler, I worked all along the waterfront. I'll pick you up in half an hour."

He had her backed into a corner. With only thirty minutes, there was no way she could get ahead of him. "I'll be ready," she said.

Montana started to lower the phone, then changed his mind. "By the way, Katie, I agree with you."

"About what?"

"That message you left on my mirror, the morning after we were together. I do still owe you."

"Oh." She'd forgotten about the message. She hadn't forgotten about their making love. "I didn't think you noticed."

"I noticed. I just haven't figured out what to do about it yet. I'm thinking of a new challenge. Double or nothing."

"Sorry, gambling man. I've made my last bet."

Katie dashed downstairs and retrieved her gym bag from her car. She ducked into the ladies' room to change. Leotards and a big shirt might not be what she would have chosen, but anything was better than a red skirt. Throwing her working clothes into the bag, she dashed barefoot up the steps with the bag in one hand and her battered gym shoes in the other.

She made it out front just as Montana pulled under the hospital canopy. She pitched the bag in the back and got in the car, tugging on a pair of thick white socks and her walking shoes.

"I liked you in the black socks better," Montana drawled.

"What black—oh." She remembered. His black socks, that first night.

"I liked the red skirt, too. What happened to it?" Montana asked as he pulled away from the door.

"Nothing. I just thought these were better swamp clothes. Where do we find a pirate ship?"

"Pirate ships sail. I guess I forget to tell you. For this trip we move by pole power."

"I don't believe we're doing this," Katie said, blowing a wisp of hair as she swatted gnats away from her face. "There must be a road."

"If so, I haven't been able to find it on any map," Montana said.

"What makes you think you can even find the place by water?"

He reached forward with the pole, propelling the pirogue along. "I'll find it, Katie. Don't worry."

"I can't help but worry. How many times have you been out in the bayou in a flat-bottomed boat?" she asked, concern etched across her face.

"Never. All my boating has been on the Mississippi."

"In a pirogue?"

"No," he admitted with a grin. "But I can do this."

She twisted her body, looking behind them as if she expected to see someone there.

"Be still," Montana said. "These things can turn over in a flash."

"Sorry. How long do you think it will take us to get there?"

"Now, that I don't know. These waterways change constantly, and it's been ten years since Cat came here. We don't know what we'll find ahead."

"I know. Oh, Montana, suppose . . . suppose . . ."

"No supposing. At the moment the waterway only goes in one direction. If we keep going, we're bound to get there."

"Maybe, but I hope you know that these swamps are full of alligators—hungry alligators. And there are more snakes out here than people."

"We're only looking for two people, Leon and Carson," Montana snapped as his pole stuck in mud for a moment, jerking the boat around. "I'm sorry, Katie," he said. "I know this is scary."

"No. I'm okay. I can do this."

He'd known that. She was scared and she was worried. If Leon was responsible for Carson's disappearance, Carson could be in danger from more than alligators and snakes.

Katie gripped the sides of the flat-bottomed boat

and ducked a low-hanging limb. The flutter of leaves frightened a bird from the marshy bank. It let out a cry of anger and flew away, setting off a cacophony of protests from the other swamp creatures being disturbed.

Though they were shaded from the sun, the day got warmer, the air heavier. The humidity increased steadily, as did the clouds, until the sky overhead was almost covered. Katie looked at her watch. "We've been at this for two hours. Don't you want me to take the pole?"

Montana shook his head. "No, but if you happen to have a candy bar in your pocket, I missed breakfast."

He looked tired. Perspiration dripped down his muscular arms and rolled down his cheeks. He hadn't shaved, his day-old beard giving him a sinister look that would have made Katie think twice about crossing him. The front of his knit shirt was wet in a V that extended from his shoulders to his belt buckle. Gaspard might have been the pirate, but Montana looked every inch the part.

At that moment they reached a fork in the waterway. Montana anchored the boat with his pole and studied the terrain. "What do you think? Left or right?"

"Don't you know?"

"Nope. In the rain all these bayous look alike."

"But it isn't raining," Katie said as the rain suddenly found its way through the trees in a torrent.

The only good thing about the rain was that it quickly became clear which directin they wanted, the section that moved swiftly and clearly, the old canal. Montana poled the pirogue to the left, into a channel that soon began to widen. They passed a clearing where dead cypress tilted crazily.

"This is right," Katie said quietly, as if she didn't want to disturb anyone. "Cat said Dario called this place the graveyard of the swamp."

At that moment a large gator slid into the black water and swam toward them as if he were the sentry on duty. A finger of land jutted out. A large water-oak tree with graceful limbs hung heavy with slate-colored moss blocked their view temporarily.

As they rounded the tree they saw it, a gray-green building that almost disappeared into the surrounding growth. There was a dock and a path to the veranda. A dog began to bark, bringing several men into view, one wearing a light gray seersucker suit.

"The man in gray," Katie said.

"Old Louis himself," Montana murmured. "Listen, Katie, I don't think he's gonna be too pleased to see us. You'd better let me do the talking."

"Nonsense. I can speak for myself," Katie said. "I—" She recognized one of the men. "Carson!"

Montana barely touched the pier before Katie jumped out and ran toward her brother, leaving him and the boat behind. "You're all right? He hasn't harmed you?"

Carson put his arms around her and hugged her. "Harmed me? No, Katie. Leon may have saved my life."

Katie pulled back and looked up at the brother she'd never expected to see again, blinking her eyelashes to keep out the rain. His sandy hair had been neatly cut.

He was clean-shaven, and until he hugged her, his clothes were sharply pressed.

"I don't understand. You said you were no good, that you were going away. I thought that you . . . you . . ."

"That I was going to do away with myself? I might have if Leon hadn't shanghaied me and brought me here."

"Well, it's all over now," Katie said. "We'll get you out of here and back to the plantation."

"First, let's get out of the rain." He slipped his arm around her shoulders and turned her toward the house.

"Oh! Carson, I've been so worried." She stopped and caught her lower lip between her teeth. "I don't know how to tell you, but we don't own Carithers' Chance any longer."

Carson's expression was very serious when he said, "What happened?" He stopped and looked back at Montana, who was tying the boat to the dock. "Did Montana claim it?"

"No, I didn't," Montana said, stepping up on the pier behind Carson. "What are you doing out here?"

"I thought I wouldn't be found," Carson said defensively. "I should have known if anyone could, it would be you. What are *you* doing here?"

"We came," Katie said, "to get you. I'm sorry if you're upset about that."

"I'm not. I'm just not ready yet to face you."

"Don't worry, Carson. Nothing could be any worse than my losing the house."

"What do you mean, you losing the house? I figured Montana called in my IOUs."

"Montana didn't claim it. I . . . I lost it. In a poker game."

Katie held her breath. Never, in a million years, would she ever have thought she'd hear those words come out of her mouth.

Carson laughed. "Good!" he exclaimed, and turned from Katie to Montana. "I hope you got your money first."

"Good?" Katie was confused. "What do you mean good? Did you understand what I told you? I went out gambling and lost. We no longer own Carithers' Chance."

"I heard you. You bet the farm and lost it. Good."

Carson tucked Katie's arm beneath his. "Come and meet Leon and the rest of his houseguests. You're invited for tea."

The setting was straight out of *The Great Gatsby*.

At the end of the veranda sat a round table with a lace tablecloth and platters of tiny sandwiches, a silver tea service, and china cups. The other guests, all men, lounged around the porch. They seemed pleasant, though reserved.

The man in the gray suit stepped forward. "I'm Louis Gaspard, your host." Gallantly, he kissed Katie's hand and shook Montana's. "Let me get you some dry clothing."

"Don't worry about it, Mr. Gaspard," Katie said.

"We were already soaking wet from the humidity. Besides, we'll just get wet again. We appreciate your hospitality," she went on in a rush, "but we'd really like to get back. Are you ready to leave, Carson?"

"No, Katie," he said patiently. "I'm not leaving just yet. It wouldn't be smart."

She was bewildered, but after what she'd been through, she wasn't about to back down. "I don't understand. If this man is holding more IOUs from you, Carson, we can deal with him."

"There are no IOUs, Miss Carithers," Leon said gently. "Come and have tea and let me explain."

Montana moved back, leaning against the side of the house. Katie had to play this out, whatever was going on. She allowed herself to be moved to a white wicker chair with bright yellow print cushions. Mr. Gaspard poured and brought her a cup of tea.

"What can I get you, Mr. Montana?" Leon asked.

"I'd like something cold—a beer," he decided.

"Sorry," Leon answered, "we serve no alcoholic beverages here." He picked up a platter and turned back to Katie. "I could prepare some lemonade."

"No! And no sandwiches or napkins or anything else you have. I'm waiting for an explanation. What's going on here?" Katie demanded.

"Katie," Montana began, coming to stand behind her.

"You're right," Leon interrupted. "I suppose I have no choice. As you may have heard, several years ago my son, Dario, died in a fire. It was called an accidental death, but he died because he was an alchoholic, a gambler, and finally a drug addict. I was so caught up in my business that I closed my eyes to his problems until it was too late. Since then, I've tried, in my own way, to make up for that by doing for others what I couldn't do for him."

Katie closed her eyes, her mind trying to fasten on what he was saying.

"I find young men, like Carson, who are heading for disaster and bring them here to a place they can't easily leave. But—and you must understand—they aren't forced to come. They only have to agree to three stipulations. They must stay for six months, agree to counseling and group therapy, and keep the location of this place a secret. We've managed to do that, until today."

"A rehabilitation center?" Montana said.

"I prefer to call it a sanctuary," Leon explained. "My concern has been for the addicts, not those left behind. By keeping it hidden, I can operate it as I choose, without interference from rules and regulations, and the people here can't be rescued or run away without risking their lives."

"But I was so worried," Katie said, beginning to see the growing uncertainty in the eyes of the other guests. "I didn't mean to give your location away."

"I see that now," the old man agreed. "Perhaps, since you have penetrated our haven today, I will have to rethink my expectations."

"I can promise you we won't tell anyone about this place," Katie assured him. "And I do thank you for rescuing my brother, but I think we can get help for his problem."

"No, Katie," Carson said. "I'm not leaving here."

"Are you sure?" she asked. "There are all kinds of good doctors associated with the hospital. I could—"

"Katie," Montana began.

"No." Carson shook him off. "No, Katie. I'll do this myself. By myself. Out here. No more having big sister bail me out. Now drink your tea and let Montana take you back to town."

"Not in that pirogue," Mr. Gaspard said. "I think you made it just in time."

Katie looked up to see the last corner of the flatboat sink leisurely beneath the murky water.

"I already know that Katie's a world-class swimmer," Montana said, "but I don't look forward to any close encounters with a gator. Any chance the limo is free?"

It was. And there was a road, artfully concealed, but present. The driver made no attempt to hide their path, and since he couldn't speak, there was no asking where they were.

Katie was lost in her own thoughts, and nothing Montana said drew her out. She was grateful when he finally stopped trying. The return trip was long and strained.

Back at Carithers' Chance, Montana insisted on escorting her to the door. "I'm glad you found your brother. Maybe he's on his way to the kind of life you want for him."

"Yes. Thank you for your help," she said.

"You're welcome."

Montana's tone had gone as flat as Katie's. A part of her regretted the feeling of separation that had come between them, but she didn't have the strength to change it. In her attempt to protect Carson, she'd lost Carithers' Chance, and he didn't even care. She supposed that all things considered, it was for the best. Carson's gambling debts would be wiped away. The burden of the plantation would be on someone else's shoulders. And Montana would no longer be a part of her life.

"Katie . . ." He seemed hesitant. "There's one more thing. About the plantation. It won't be transferred to Jonah right away. He's agreed to having the fund-raiser here."

Now it was Katie's turn to hesitate. Montana was still looking after her. She had to stop that and there was only one way to let him off the hook and maintain any dignity. "Thank you. I'll start looking for a place to live. And Montana, I . . ." She took a deep breath and gave a short prayer that she could go through with what she was about to say. "I . . . I don't know any other way to do it but to say, you were right."

"I was right? About what?"

"That first night we met, in your cabin, the night I won your boat . . ."

He'd been waiting for her to bring it up. Knowing Katie, and he thought now that he did, she'd never welsh or leave a loose end.

"Don't worry about it," he began, "I'm not—"

"No!" She cut him off. "You were right all along. I'm going to say this once, then never again. I cheated. I didn't win the boat. So, I'm not sure where you and I stand, money-wise, I mean. But you figure it out and let me know."

He took a step closer. "You cheated?"

"That's what I said. I couldn't end this without telling you the truth."

He merely looked at her, too stunned to speak. He'd made up his mind that what she'd done that first night had been a glorious sacrifice for her brother. Then he'd fallen in love. No matter what Katie was saying, she hadn't cheated. And he knew without a doubt that she was lying now. She was giving his life back to him, forcing him to accept it. Katie, so determined to save her family and her land, was saying good-bye to both. It had to be because she cared—for him.

"Thank you, Katie," Montana said. "I know how hard it was for you to tell me. Life dealt us both a tough hand. But we played it out, didn't we?"

"I suppose."

Montana lifted her chin with one finger. "What about it, my lady in red? One final kiss? For luck?"

She must have nodded, for seconds later the heat of his lips touched hers for one urgent, hungry moment. And then he was gone, leaving her leaning against the door of a past that had just been closed.

TEN

Katie listened to the hollow sounds of Montana's footsteps as he walked off the porch. Every footfall carried the man she loved further out of her life.

And there was nothing she could do. From the first she'd told him that her family and her plantation were the only important things in her life. Now both were gone and what did she have?

Empty arms and lost dreams.

The night they'd made love she'd covered her need with a lie—that she wanted him for one night only. She hadn't known then how foolish she'd been. A house was just a house. Her parents were gone, and Carson? The thought of her brother made her first sad, then happy. He was free.

This Louis Gaspard had been able to do what she hadn't. No, not Mr. Gaspard, Carson. He'd been the one to take his life back, to start again and find a new direction.

Wasn't that what she'd wanted?

Yes. She just hadn't expected that Carson's freedom would take him away from her. For the first time in her life she, too, was free.

Why then did she feel as if her heart was shattered into a thousand pieces?

Because in getting what she thought she wanted, she'd lost the one thing Mary Katherine Carithers never allowed herself to honestly need. Someone to love her.

She heard the sound of the car engine as it roared to life and the spray of gravel as Montana tore off into the night. Full speed ahead, just as he always drove. Facing danger head-on. Never in doubt. Always sure of himself. A man who knew what he wanted and went after it.

She sighed and started up the stairs. It was just as well. Under other circumstances, she might have gone after him. The lady in red would have. But she was just Katie Carithers, and her heart hurt for what might have been.

Cat Boulineau's dark eyes flashed. Her red fingernails drummed the top of Katie's desk as she struggled for words. "You told him you cheated?"

"I did. It was the only thing to do. Anything else would have . . . complicated matters."

"And things aren't complicated now?"

"No. I'm looking for an apartment. And after the charity fund-raiser, I'll sign the house over to Big Jonah. Carson will stay at Mr. Gaspard's. When he's ready, he'll find a teaching job. I'll keep working here at the hospital, and life will get back to normal."

"All tied up in a neat little package, huh?"

"I hope so."

Cat simply shook her head. "I don't understand you, Katie. You're simply going to walk away from the most exciting man you've ever met? You aren't even going to let him know that you're in love with him?"

Katie came to her feet and walked to the window. "I'm not."

"Rats! Of course you are. I've watched you take care of everybody and everything in your family for years—except Katie. Now Katie has a chance to have someone care about her and you're just giving up?"

"I'm not giving up, Cat. I'm not—I mean—I can't—"

"Can't fall in love? Too late, girl. You're already there. Admit it. You've fallen in love with Rhett Butler Montana."

Katie leaned her forehead against the windowpane. "Yes. I've fallen in love with Rhett Butler Montana. But I'll get over it."

"Maybe, but I don't know why you'd want to."

"Because he doesn't love me," Katie whispered. "He can't. We're too different."

"Well, you could have fooled me. The way he's been running all over the country helping you look for Carson makes me think he might be interested. Of course, I don't know. Most men would probably do that, wouldn't they?"

"But he's a gambler, Cat. He's used to taking risks, betting on the future. If he loses, he'll just bet again."

"Look, Katie. If you've learned one thing in the last six years, you ought to know that all life's a gamble. The question is whether the pot is big enough to take the risk."

"I guess I'm just scared," Katie admitted. "I could fight for Carson, but for me? I don't know how."

"Maybe Katie Carithers is scared, but Montana's lady in red isn't. For once in your life, Katie, go after what you want."

Katie turned slowly around. "What makes you think I can do it?"

Cat waited a long time before answering. "You'll never know, will you? Unless you try."

"You're right, Cat. Let's go shopping."

"Again? What about the office? Who's going to run the show?"

"I'm in charge," Katie said, straightening her shoulders. "I figure the hospital owes me a couple of years in overtime. Let it take care of itself for an hour."

"What are we shopping for this time?" Cat asked, hurrying to keep up with her boss.

"A dress and a mask."

"Anything special in mind?" Cat asked.

"Very special. It has to be something red."

"Still sounds crazy to me, Montana," Big Jonah said as he signed the legal form spread out on Montana's desk. "I've seen that old house, and it's practically falling down on its foundation."

"Just sign the paper, Jonah. I want to make certain you're relinquishing any claim to Carithers' Chance before I pay off Katie's debt."

Big Jonah leaned over and scrawled his signature with a flourish. "There. It's done."

"And," Montana said in a voice that brooked no argument, "you'll never gamble with anybody named Carithers again."

"You got it."

Montana turned to Royal, who hovered in the background. "Give him the money, Royal."

Royal shook his head and counted out the bills.

Jonah gathered them up, stuck them in his jacket pocket, and held out his hand. "Pleasure to do business with you, Montana. I'll gamble with you anytime."

Royal closed the office door behind Jonah and turned back to face Montana. "You know you could have talked him down on the amount, don't you?"

"I didn't want to give him any grounds for reneging."

"So now you own a plantation. What are your plans, boss?"

"The only plans I have right now are to rent a tux and a mask."

"You mean one of those with the stripe down the pant leg and a pleated shirt?"

"That's exactly what I mean," Montana agreed. "Where can I find one?"

"Ask Cat, she'll know."

"Sure you don't want to go to the ball?"

"Not me," Royal said. "I got a gambling boat to run."

"Oh, and Royal," Montana said with a half smile. "Get yourself a black frock coat and string tie, will you?"

"You mean you're asking me to join the Earp gang?"

"As of tonight," Montana said, "you're in charge of it."

The night was perfect for Halloween. Dark clouds swept across the sky in a water-filled smear of boiling black. The limos glided up to the door, dislodged their glamorous occupants, and moved away.

Katie was grateful that in the eerie shadows, Carithers' Chance didn't show its shabby exterior. Inside, the elaborate decorations concealed the water-stained walls and worn carpets. The entire lower floor, as always, had been transformed into a casino. Volunteer dealers from local establishments manned the tables. Gaudy lit wheels and rented slot machines blinked, jingled, and whirled.

The covered veranda had been transformed into a dance floor with the study doubling as a bandstand. Once, the occasion had simply been a night to gamble for charity, but over the years, the guests had gradually turned it into a masquerade. Since it was Halloween, elaborate masks had become the order of the evening. The men wore more simple ones; the women wore feathers, jewels, and satin. Each patron vied for the grand prize for best mask, to be awarded at midnight.

Katie stood in the foyer, greeting each attendee. This time her red dress was long. It covered every inch of her like a shimmering skin. Her mask was a creation of feathers and sparkles. She didn't know whether or not Montana would come, but she'd made certain he'd received an invitation to the five-hundred-dollar-a-person event. She hadn't seen a check from him, but it could have come in today and she wouldn't have seen it.

By eleven o'clock her feet hurt and her heart was heavy. Cat was wrong. If Montana had been interested in her, he would have come. She gave up watching the doors and turned to the guests. The gamblers had been unusually generous tonight. Katie was certain that the hospital fund would be large. That should have made her happy, but she could barely force herself to smile.

"Hey, Katie," Cat's familiar voice called out. "Come and show these people how to play poker."

"No, I don't think so," Katie said, trying to back away. "It wouldn't be fair—proper," she amended.

"Sure it would," the head of the hospital said. "Your assistant has been telling us how good you are. I'll stake you to some chips. It's for a good cause, isn't it? We'll even let you deal."

That was when she felt his presence. Montana was here. She couldn't see him, but her body suddenly felt alive. That brief moment of intense connection rattled her so that she dropped into the empty seat without being aware that she'd done so.

Helplessly, she looked to Cat. But Cat was looking

at someone moving through the crowd toward them, someone Katie couldn't see.

"Mind if I play?" Montana stopped on the other side of the table.

"Not at all," Cat said, coming to her feet. "You can have my chair."

"No," Katie protested weakly.

"Certainly," the hospital director said. "Everybody's money is welcome here."

"Is that true?" Montana asked, his question directed at Katie. "Everyone is welcome?"

Money, Katie thought. That's why we're here. To raise money for the hospital. Without making an utter fool of herself, she had no choice but to play. And this time she wouldn't lose.

"Of course. What's your game, stranger?" she said, glad that her face was covered by a mask.

"Stud poker," he said smoothly. "If that's all right with the rest of you. I feel lucky."

The others agreed.

Katie tried not to look at him, but with him being directly across from her, she couldn't avoid it. If he'd been wicked in his riverboat-gambler attire, he was absolutely devastating in a tux. Tonight, he was a pirate, wearing a black satin mask with no adornment. Other than not revealing his name, he'd made no real attempt at concealing his identity. The chances were that most of the people here wouldn't have known him anyway.

To Katie, he seemed intent on the card game, not allowing his attention to focus on her.

To Montana, focusing on his cards was the only way

he could sit across the table from Katie and not touch her. What she'd exhibited freely before, she concealed now, with a dress that covered her arms, her neck, every inch of her—until she turned her back. There was no back. It dipped so low that she couldn't have been wearing anything beneath it.

If he'd thought the short skirt and nothing little straps had been sexy before, he'd been wrong. It took him two hands of poker to get his breathing under control.

They played four hands, the hospital head winning one, Montana winning one, and Katie taking the other two. On the fifth hand, the cards went to Montana as the dealer. He gave Katie a long searching look, reached inside his pocket, and pulled out a cellophane-wrapped deck, exactly like the one she'd brought on the *Scarlet Lady*.

"Let's have a new deck," he said, unwrapping the cards and allowing the covering to fall to the floor. "And I'd like to raise the stakes, Miss Carithers. If you're interested."

"What did you have in mind?" she managed to say.

"Why don't we make it one final hand? Double or nothing."

In her subconscious, she'd known it was coming. They'd been rushing toward this moment all night. And until she spoke, she hadn't known how she'd answer. She had nothing to give up if she lost. She had to win.

"One hand, sir. Double or nothing."

"Too rich for my pocketbook," one of the players said.

"I think I'll pass," the hospital director said.

The game would be between her and Montana. A showdown at midnight, just as it had been the first time they'd met.

Montana shuffled the cards, then held them out for Katie to cut them. She shook her head.

He dealt himself a card, facedown, then one to Katie. He took a casual look at his card, smiled. Katie did the same. The next card was exposed. A ten of hearts for Montana, a nine of spades for Katie.

Montana slid a stack of chips to the center of the table. "Ah yes. I do feel lucky."

Katie smiled, matched his bet, and added more chips. "That's good. The hospital appreciates your confidence."

The third card for Montana was a nine of clubs. "Possible straight for me." He turned over Katie's card, a ten of diamonds. "Well, now. Possible straight for the lady in red. But what is she holding?"

"It will cost you to find out. Are you betting, sir?"

"Oh, yes." He added another stack of chips to the table. "And you? Are you ready to concede?"

"Give up? Not on your life." She added chips. "I think I'll raise you another ten."

Montana tried not to grin. This was working out just the way he'd planned. Except for that dress. Even though he could only see the front, he knew her back was bare. And he could feel her skin beneath his fingertips.

"I'll match you."

"Of course you will." The crowd grew quieter, as if it knew there was more going on here than a game.

Montana dealt the fourth cards, a seven of diamonds to himself and the eight of hearts to Katie. Katie looked at the table. Ten, nine, and seven to Montana. Ten, nine, and eight to her. When had she ever seen two such similar hands before? Could Montana's hole card possibly be an eight? She was beginning to have a funny feeling about what she was seeing.

He turned over his last card. She'd been wrong. The hole card wasn't an eight, the card he just dealt himself was. Now he was showing seven, eight, nine, and ten. How could that be? He bet, shoving the rest of his chips into the pot.

"An unusual fall to the cards, don't you think?" she observed. "I don't suppose my last card would be a seven, would it?"

"I sincerely hope not, darling," he said, "but one never knows." He turned over her card and placed it on the table. The seven of clubs. "Well, well. If I weren't dealing, I'd question these hands."

Katie studied the cards and swallowed hard. Concealing her nerves would have been impossible without the mask. Once again she checked her hole card, just to make sure she hadn't forgotten. This time she took a better look, sliding her finger tips across the top and sides as if she were trying to decide what to do.

Then she felt it, the tiny nick in the corner of the card. She'd been right. It was the same deck, the one he'd threatened her with, the one he'd said he locked away in his safe to use as evidence against her. He'd come here prepared to cheat to win. What was he doing?

"I think I'll just bet it all," he said. "After all, it's for a good cause." He shoved the rest of his chips forward, reached into his coat, and pulled out a stack of bills, which he added to the pot. "I believe the bet is double or nothing?"

He must know that she couldn't keep up with him. She didn't have enough chips left to cover his cash. She was going to lose the director's money to Montana. Even with the cut of it to the charity, she'd still lose her stake.

"Let's see what we have here. Looks like there's about five thousand dollars in the pot, wouldn't you say? Double that would make it ten."

Katie gulped. There was no way she could cover that. What to do? If she folded, the stake was gone. If she went with the bet and lost, she'd be back where she started, but she had nothing to cover her losses. Besides that, the deck was marked. Montana knew what she had. If he was going to cheat, she'd find her own way to match his bet.

"Can't handle it, darling?" he asked.

"Not unless you'll accept my personal IOU."

"Oh? And what would that be?"

"Would it matter?"

"Not as long as it covered your bet."

She paused a long moment. "Will someone get me a piece of paper and a pen?"

Seconds later Katie had written something on the

paper, folded it, and slid it to the center of the table. "Will you trust me on this?"

"Of course. But let me make a suggestion," he drawled, pulling the familiar cheroot from an inner pocket and clasping it between his teeth.

"I'm listening."

"Instead of double or nothing, if you win, you get the pot for the hospital. I don't have the cash with me to double it, but I'll throw in the contents of this envelope to make up the rest, with one stipulation. The envelope goes to you personally. Will you trust me, Kate?"

Did she trust him? It was simple. "Yes. But if I lose, the hospital loses?"

"No. I wouldn't do that. In either case, the money goes to charity. If you lose, I get you—forever."

The suggestion was outrageous. Montana knew it and so did Katie. He was challenging her. Katie Carithers's family name against that of a professional gambler. How much did she trust him? What was she willing to give? What did she want forever?

There was a collective gasp around the table. "Now wait a minute," the director began. "I don't think you need to do something like that, Katie."

A warm flush spread over her. Montana had set the game up from the beginning so she'd lose. Why else would he bring a marked deck? And there was nothing she could do about it. What was even more astounding was, she didn't want to.

"It's for charity, isn't it? I think that's an acceptable idea, sir. I'd just like to make one small change in the bid, if I may."

"Of course. What would you change?"

"If I win, instead of the contents of the envelope, the lady in red gets you—forever."

Montana let out a devilish laugh. "My lady in red, if you win, you get both. Let's see what you have."

She turned over her hole card, revealing the jack of spades.

Montana looked at her for a long minute. Everyone around the table held their breath. Katie waited, pulse pounding, her heart in her throat. Finally, Montana slid his cards together and looked across the table.

"You win," he said.

The table went into an uproar. Onlookers slapping Katie on the back, the director beaming from ear to ear, Cat fighting back a look of disbelief.

"I'll just take care of our collateral," Montana said, claiming the envelope and the paper and replacing them inside his coat pocket. "According to your conditions, I belong to you." He held out his hand. "Will you dance with me?"

"Yes," she agreed. Anything to get away from the eyes of all those who were hearing about their bet. Moments later they were beyond the gambling areas. Montana slid his arm around her waist and pulled her close.

"I've wanted to do this ever since I watched you dance with René," he said, holding her close.

"Montana, what did all that mean, back there?" Katie asked, realizing as she did that the question was foolish.

"We gambled. You won."

"But what are you doing now?"

"I'm dancing with my lady." And he was finding out that he was right about the dress. There was nothing underneath.

Katie knew she ought to be asking more questions, but she couldn't seem to think what she wanted to know. The moonlight, shining through the trees, cast lacy spears of light across the grounds.

The music was romantic. The man holding her was wickedly handsome and her feet felt as if they had wings. Katie gave a little moan.

"What's wrong, darling?"

"Nothing. It's just that in all the years we've had the ball here, I've never danced the last dance. And this is the last dance, isn't it? Last dance at Carithers' Chance."

"You never know," Montana said, planting a kiss behind her ear. "You just never know."

At that moment the music stopped, the drummer gave an attention-getting roll, and the crowd grew quiet. The hospital director, with Cat at his side, took the microphone.

First he gave out the awards for the most spectacular masks. Then he asked for another drumroll, followed with: "And I'd like to announce that the preliminary figures appear to be at least a third more than last year's total. But what is even more exciting is a special donation to the hospital in the name of the Stewart family of Charleston, South Carolina, by their son. Will Mr. Stewart please come forward."

Everybody looked around, puzzled expressions on their faces.

Katie turned toward Montana. "The Stewart family of Charleston, South Carolina?"

"Well," he explained as he took her hand and started toward the podium, "like you said, family is important. If I'm going to marry a Carithers, I'd better do something to make peace with mine."

Her feet and legs responded, though she would never have made it had it not been for Montana's strong arm around her.

Amid ear-shattering applause, Montana and Katie took their places on the platform. "You're asking me to marry you?" Katie asked, her voice carrying through the sound system.

"Of course, darling. If you'll have me. What do you think forever means?"

"Are you Mr. Stewart?" the hospital administrator asked incredulously. "Of the Charleston Stewarts?"

Katie stepped forward, bringing Montana with her. "Yes. I mean, no. The man who made the donation is Mr. Rhett Butler Montana, the man I'm going to marry."

She pulled off her mask and turned toward him. This was the biggest gamble of her life. There was no tomorrow. "Are you sure, Montana?"

"Why, Miss Katherine," he said, ripping his mask from his face, "you won me fair and square. You know Montana always makes good on his bets."

Then, before half the old blood of Louisiana and a good portion of the new, he kissed her.

Only when he finally let her go did he hear the small

voice whispering in his ear. "You scoundrel, I know the truth."

"The truth, Kate? Whatever do you mean?"

"Those cards were marked. You cheated."

"Sure I did. Are you going to tell?"

"Not in a million years."

It was later, much later that night, when Rhett slid out of bed and emptied his jacket pocket. He handed Katie the envelope and a small box. "I love you, Katie. This is my wedding gift to you."

She sat up in the bed and leaned back against the padded headboard, pulling the sheet over her bare breasts and tucking it beneath her arms. "But we're not married yet."

"We will be, just soon as you and Cat can shop for a dress."

"Does it have to be red?" she asked seriously.

"Come to think of it, forget the dress, just open your present so we can get back to the honeymoon."

Katie opened the envelope, unfolded the legal document inside, and felt her eyes fill with tears. "A clear title to Carithers' Chance? You paid off Jonah? How did you do that?"

"Well, I do have a little problem with that. I'm going to need your signature."

"On what?"

"On a bill of sale?"

"What bill of sale?" she asked.

"For the *Scarlet Lady*."

Katie leaned forward, allowing the sheet to fall to her waist. "You can't sell the *Lady*."

"Why not?"

"Because—because I own her, or did you forget?"

Montana took her hand in his and raised it to his lips. "No you don't, Katie. We own her."

"I'm telling you one last time, Rhett Butler Montana Stewart, I didn't cheat."

"I know. But I opened the paper, your collateral on the bet. You signed the boat over to me, win or lose. This will just make everything nice and legal. Open the little box."

She looked at the box, wrapped in red foil and tied with a glittery bow. "You knew?"

"I know you didn't cheat. You may be the best poker player I know and I'm never going to play with you again—at least not poker."

Katie slipped the ribbon off the package and the paper fell to the bed. She removed the top and gasped. Inside the tissue was a small fluff of white. "Cotton? This is cotton."

"Yep, the kind of cotton we're going to grow on Carithers' Chance, once we sell the boat and buy back the land."

"You want to grow cotton?" She couldn't hide her surprise.

"Yes, ma'am. I always did. I just wanted to do it for the wrong reasons. Now I want to sit on my veranda with a baby on each knee, a mint julep in my hand, and my beautiful wife at my side."

Katie looked at her wicked lover and smiled. She

reached into the drawer of her night table and pulled out a deck of cards. "I'm not sure I trust you, Montana. Cut the cards. High card decides how many children we have."

He took the deck and shuffled the cards, letting them fly into the air. "I told you, no more gambling, Katie. I love you. To me, forever is a sure thing."

She reached out and put her hand on his leg. "You really mean it, don't you?"

"I do. You've filled all the dark places in my life and given me a future. Tell me that you love me, Katie. I want to hear the words."

"I do. I love you. You've given me my past and a future I never expected. I'll marry you whenever and wherever you want. We'll drink mint juleps, grow cotton, and make babies." Her hand began to move forward. "What do you say to that?"

"Ah, my lady in red, I can say with certainty that the South's going to rise again."

EPILOGUE

Lincoln McAllister rarely left Shangri-la. But no one was more surprised than he when he decided to attend Montana and Katie's wedding at Carithers' Chance.

His decision seemed more and more improbable as he drove his rented car up River Road toward the plantation. For years he'd had an assistant, but thus far, he'd never left him completely in charge. To relieve his guilt, Mac turned on his portable phone, though he genuinely hoped it wouldn't ring.

It was late November. He'd called Sterling, just to check on Conner and his new bride, and casually inquired, "Are you going to the wedding?"

"Oh, no," she'd answered. "I can't."

"Please come," he'd said. "After all, you're partially responsible for the wedding. I'm certain they'd love it if you came."

"Perhaps," she said softly. "We'll see."

"Perhaps," he repeated now, out loud. Such an old-fashioned word. He wondered what she looked like, this woman who rarely went out. Well, perhaps he'd know soon. If she came.

According to the map, he was almost there. Then the phone rang.

"Mac, here."

"Mac? This is Conner. I've got a problem."

"What is it?"

"It's Sterling," he said.

Mac felt his chest contract. "Sterling? What's wrong?"

"She's disappeared."

THE EDITORS' CORNER

It's hard to believe that autumn is here! Soon Old Man Winter will be making his way down our paths, and we'll all be complaining about the cold weather instead of the oppressive heat. One thing you won't be complaining about is the Loveswept November lineup. And trust us, Old Man Winter doesn't stand a chance with these sexy men on the prowl!

Timing is everything, so they say, and Suzanne Brockmann proves the old adage true with her next LOVESWEPT, #858, **TIME ENOUGH FOR LOVE**. Chuck Della Croce has a problem. His time machine is responsible for a tragedy that has resulted in the deaths of hundreds. Thinking he can go back in time to literally save the world, Chuck ends up on Maggie Winthrop's doorstep. Maggie can't help but notice the stranger who's obnoxiously banging on her door, especially since he's naked as a jaybird! When he tells her he's from the future, she's ready to call the men in white coats, but something about him gives her pause. As Chuck explains his mission to prevent a disaster and save her life, Maggie must learn to accept that anything is possible. Suzanne Brockmann guides us in a timeless journey and persuades us to believe in the powers of destiny and second chances.

Eyes meeting across a crowded room, sexual tension building to a crescendo . . . *bam!*, you've got yourself a Loveswept! That certainly is the recipe conjured up in LOVESWEPT #859, **RELATIVE STRANGERS**, by Kathy Lynn Emerson. A ghost is lurking in the halls of Sinclair House, one who is anxious to reunite with her own true love. But first she must bring together the hearts of Lucas Sinclair and Corrie Ballantyne. Unfortunately, the two won't cooperate. Strange occurrences involving Corrie keep happening at Lucas's historic hotel, and he needs to get to the bottom of things before the place goes under. After seeing the ghosts of Lucas's ancestors, Corrie must decide if it's her own desire that draws her to him, or if it's the will of another. Can Corrie make peace with the past by unearthing hidden truths and soothing the unspoken sorrows of the man she will love forever? Kathy Lynn Emerson's exquisitely romantic ghost story is downright irresistible in both its sensuality and its mystery.

Trapped on an island with a hurricane on the loose, Trevor Fox and Jana Jenkins seek **SHELTER FROM THE STORM**, LOVESWEPT #860 by Maris Soule. Cursing a storm that had grounded all his charters, Trevor was only too glad to agree to lend a hand to the alluring seductress with the pouty lips.

Little did he know that his day would go from bad to worse, and from there to . . . well, whatever comes after that. Held at gunpoint, he is forced to fly to the Bahamas, and into the path of a hurricane. Jana Jenkins just wants to live a quiet, uneventful life, but when her stepbrother is kidnapped, Jana does what's necessary to save him—even if that includes dragging this brash pirate with a tarnished reputation along for the ride. Loveswept veteran Maris Soule knows there's nothing like a little danger to spice up the lives of a woman on the run and a man who enjoys the chase!

Dr. Kayla Davies learns just what will be her **ULTIMATE SURRENDER**, LOVESWEPT #861 by Jill Shalvis, an author who is penning her way into our hearts. When Kayla and her ex–brother-in-law, Ryan Scott, are summoned to the home of a beloved aunt, the two must make peace with their past and with each other. There's no love lost between the ruthless police detective and Kayla, but Ryan can't understand the fear he sees lurking in the depths of her blue eyes. As Kayla grows to know Ryan, she finds herself in the strange position of being both attracted and repelled by the man she once believed evil. Trapped in a web of old deceits, Ryan and Kayla struggle together to silence the ghosts of their past. But if Kayla dares to confess her dark secret, can Ryan find the strength to forgive? Writing with touching emotion and tender sensuality, Jill Shalvis once again proves that love can be a sweet victory over heartbreak.

Happy reading!

With warmest regards,

Susann Brailey   Joy Abella

Susann Brailey   Joy Abella

Senior Editor   Administrative Editor

P.S. Look for these Bantam women's fiction titles coming in November. From national bestselling author Kay Hooper comes **FINDING LAURA**, available in hardcover. A collector of mirrors, struggling artist Laura Sutherland stumbles across an antique hand mirror that lands her in the midst of the powerful Kilbourne family and a legacy of deadly intent. Leslie LaFoy makes her Bantam debut with **IT HAPPENED ONE NIGHT**. Allana Chapman was not prepared for the travel through time, and Kiervan des Marceaux must protect her in order to fulfill the prophecy and Allana's destiny as the Seer of the Find. Now available in paperback from *New York Times* bestselling author Sandra Brown is **HAWK O'TOOLE'S HOSTAGE**, a riveting contemporary romance about a woman who is held hostage by a desperate man . . . and a desperate desire. And immediately following this page, preview the Bantam women's fiction titles on sale in September.

For current information on Bantam's women's fiction, visit our new Web site, *Isn't It Romantic*, at the following address:

http://www.bdd.com/romance

Don't miss these extraordinary books
by your favorite Bantam authors!

On sale in September:

AFTER CAROLINE
by Kay Hooper

WHEN YOU WISH . . .
**by Jane Feather, Patricia Coughlin,
Sharon & Tom Curtis, Elizabeth Elliott,
Patricia Potter, and Suzanne Robinson**

THE BARGAIN
by Jane Ashford

THE CHALICE AND
THE BLADE
by Glenna McReynolds

AFTER CAROLINE

BY KAY HOOPER

"Kay Hooper is a master storyteller."
—Tami Hoag

Two women who look enough alike to be twins. Both in-volved in car wrecks at the same time. One survives, one doesn't.

Now, plagued by a bewildering connection to a woman she never knew, driven by an urgent compulsion she doesn't understand, Joanna Flynn travels three thousand miles across the country to the picturesque town where Caroline McKenna lived—and mysteriously died. There Joanna will run into a solid wall of suspicion as she searches for the truth: Was Caroline's death an accident? Or was she the target of a killer willing to kill again?

"You're sure you're okay? No pain anywhere?"

"Not even a twinge." She looked past his shoulder to watch other motorists slipping and sliding down the bank toward her, and swallowed hard when she saw just how far her car had rolled. "My God. I should be dead, shouldn't I?"

Jim looked back and briefly studied the wide path of flattened brush and churned-up earth, then returned his gaze to her and smiled. "Like I said, this seems to be your lucky day."

Joanna looked once more at the car crumpled so snugly around her, and shivered. As close as she ever wanted to come . . .

Within five minutes, the rescue squad and para-medics arrived, all of them astonished but pleased to find her unhurt. Jim backed away to allow the rescue people room to work, joining the throng of onlookers scattered down the bank, and Joanna realized only then that she was the center of quite a bit of attention.

"I always wanted to be a star," she murmured.

The nearest paramedic, a brisk woman of about Joanna's age wearing a name badge that said E. Mallory, chuckled in response. "Word's gotten around that you haven't a scratch. Don't be surprised if the fourth estate shows up any minute."

Joanna was about to reply to that with another light comment, but before she could open her mouth, the calm of the moment was suddenly, terribly, shattered. There was a sound like a gunshot, a dozen voices screamed, *"Get back!"* and Joanna turned her gaze toward the windshield to see what looked like a thick black snake with a fiery head falling toward her out of the sky.

Then something slammed into her with the unbelievable force of a runaway train, and everything went black.

There was no sense of time passing, and Joanna didn't feel she had gone somewhere else. She felt . . . suspended, in a kind of limbo. Weightless, content, she drifted in a peaceful silence. She was waiting for something, she knew that. Waiting to find out something. The silence was absolute, but gradually the darkness began to abate, and she felt a gentle tug. She turned, or thought she did, and moved in the direction of the soft pull.

But almost immediately, she was released, drifting once more as the darkness deepened again. And she had a sudden sense that she was not alone, that someone shared the darkness with her. She felt a featherlight touch, so fleeting she wasn't at all sure of it, as though someone or something had brushed past her.

Don't let her be alone.

Joanna heard nothing, yet the plea was distinct in her mind, and the emotions behind it were nearly overwhelming. She tried to reach out toward that other, suffering presence, but before she could, something yanked at her sharply.

"Joanna? Joanna! Come on, Joanna, open your eyes!"

That summons was an audible one, growing louder as she felt herself pulled downward. She resisted for an instant, reluctant, but then fell in a rush until she felt the heaviness of her own body once more.

Instantly, every nerve and muscle she possessed seemed on fire with pain, and she groaned as she forced open her eyes.

A clear plastic cup over her face, and beyond it a circle of unfamiliar faces breaking into grins. And beyond *them* a clear blue summer sky decorated with fleecy white clouds. She was on the ground. What was she doing on the ground?

"She's back with us," one of the faces said back over his shoulder to someone else. "Let's get her on the stretcher." Then, to her, "You're going to be all right, Joanna. You're going to be just fine."

Joanna felt her aching body lifted. She watched dreamily as she floated past more faces. Then a vaguely familiar one appeared, and she saw it say something to her, something that sunk in only some time later as she rode in a wailing ambulance.

Definitely your lucky day. You almost died twice.

Her mind clearing by that time, Joanna could only agree with Jim's observation. How many people, after all, go through one near-death experience? Not many. Yet here she was, whole and virtually unharmed—if you discounted the fact that the only part of her body that didn't ache was the tip of her nose.

Still, she was very much alive, and incredibly grateful.

At the hospital, she was examined, soothed, and medicated. She would emerge from the day's incredible experiences virtually unscathed, the doctors told her. She had one burn mark on her right ankle where the electricity from the power line had arced between exposed metal and her flesh, and she'd be sore for a while both from the shock that had stopped her heart and from the later efforts to start it again.

She was a very lucky young lady and should suffer no lasting effects from what had happened to her; that was what they said.

But they were wrong. Because that was the night the dreams began.

When You Wish . . .

by Jane Feather, Patricia Coughlin, Sharon & Tom Curtis, Elizabeth Elliott, Patricia Potter, and Suzanne Robinson

To thine own wish be true. Do not follow the moth to the star.

So says the message in an exquisite green bottle. Is it a wish? A warning? A spell to cast over a lover? In six charming love stories, a mysterious bottle brings a touch of magic to the lives of all who possess it. . . .

The moon rode high against the soft blackness of the night sky. The great stones of the circle threw their shadows across the sleeping plain. The girl waited in the grove of trees. He had said he would come when the moon reached its zenith.

She shivered despite the warmth of the June night, drawing her woolen cloak about her. The massive pillars of Stonehenge held a menacing magic, even for one accustomed to the rites that took place within the sinister enclosure. The thought of venturing into the vast black space within the circle terrified her as it terrified all but the priests. It was forbidden ground.

Her ears were stretched for the sound of footsteps, although she knew that she would hear nothing as his sandaled feet slid over the moss of the grove. She stepped closer to the trunk of a poplar tree, then jumped back as she touched its encrustation of sacred mistletoe.

"Move into the moonlight."

Even though she'd been waiting for it, the soft command sent a thrill of fear shivering in her belly, curling her toes. She looked over her shoulder and saw him, shrouded in white, his hood pulled low over his head, only his eyes, pale blue in the darkness, gave life to the form.

The girl stepped out of the grove onto the moonlit plain. She felt him behind her. The priest who held the power of the Druid's Egg. She stopped, turned to face him. "Will you help me?"

"Are you certain you know what you're asking for?" His voice rasped, hoarse as if he'd been shouting for hours. The pale blue eyes burned in their deep sockets.

She nodded. "I am certain." With a sudden movement, she shook off her hood. Her hair cascaded down her back, a silver river in the moonlight. "Will the magic work?"

A smile flashed across his eyes and he reached out to touch her hair. "It has the power of desires and dreams."

"To make them come true?" Her voice was anxious, puzzled.

He said nothing, but drew from beneath his cloak a thick-bladed knife. "Are you ready?"

The girl swallowed, nodded her head. She turned her back to the priest. She felt him take her hair at the nape of her neck. She felt the knife sawing through the thick mass, silvered by the moon. She felt it part beneath the blade. And then she stood shorn, the night air cold on her bare neck. "Now you will give it to me?"

He was winding the hank of hair around his hand and didn't answer as he reveled in the richness of the payment. The hair of a maiden had many useful properties but it was a potent sacrifice that few young virgins were voluntarily prepared to make. He opened a leather pouch at his waist and carefully deposited the shining mass inside, before taking out an object of green glass. It lay on his flat palm.

She looked closely at it. A green glass bottle with a chased silver top. Vertical banks of chased silver flowed down the bottle from the stopper, like liquid mercury. There was something inside it. She could see the shape in the neck behind the glowing glass. Would it work? It had to work. Only the magic of a man who held the power of the Druid's Egg could enable her to make the right decision.

She reached out and touched it tentatively with her fingertip. "The spell is within?"

"You will read it within."

"What must I do? Must I open it in a certain way? Read it in a certain way?"

"You will read it as it is meant to be read." The smile was there again as he took her hand and placed the bottle on her plam. "As it is meant to be read for you," he added.

Her fingers closed over the bottle. She frowned, wondering what he could mean. A spell was a spell, surely. It could only be read one way.

When she looked up, the priest had gone.

The Druid's Egg was hatched by several serpents laboring together. When hatched it was held in the air by their hissing. The man who had given her the spell had caught the egg as it danced on the serpent's venom. He had caught it and escaped the poison himself. Such a man . . . such a priest . . . had the power to do anything.

Holding the bottle tightly in her fist, the girl turned her back on the stone pillars. She tried to walk but soon was running across the plain toward the village nestled in a fold of land beside the river that flowed to the sea. She had never seen the sea, only heard tales of vast blueness that disappeared into the sky. But the river flowing between sloping banks was her friend.

She sat down on the bank outside the village and with trembling fingers opened the bottle. A scrap of leather, carefully rolled, lay inside. She drew it out, unfurled it, held it up to the bright moonlight.

Runes were scratched into the leather at the top, and at the sight of the magic symbols her heart leaped. She hadn't sold her hair for nothing. Here was the incantation she had bought. She squinted at the strange marks and wondered what she was to do with them. Only when she turned the leather over did she see the writing in legible strokes inked onto the leather.

"To thine own wish be true. Do not follow the moth to the star."

The girl stared in disbelieving dismay. What did it mean? It told her nothing. There was nothing magic about those words. She looked again at the runes and knew in her bones that they would add nothing to the message. They were decoration for a simple truth. She thrust the scrap of leather back into the bottle and corked it.

Be true to her own wish. Was it telling her she must face the consequences of her desires? If she wished for the stars, she would burn like the moth at the candle.

Slowly, she stood up. She held her hand over the swift flowing water and opened it. The little bottle dropped, was caught by the current and whisked away toward the distant sea. As distant as the stars.

The choice was still hers to make. The road still branched before her. She had sold her hair for the druid's power and she was left, as always, with only her own.

"Jane Ashford is an exceptional talent."
—*Rendezvous*

THE BARGAIN

BY JANE ASHFORD

It's more than ridiculous, it's damned embarrassing and inconvenient . . . for a scientist with his reputation to be called in to get rid of a ghost. But when the prince regent summons Lord Alan Gresham to London to solve the mystery of a haunting, he has no choice. At least the task shouldn't take much time. He will uncover the perpetrators of the hoax and then return with speed to his experiments. Or so Gresham thinks, until he finds his calm, logical investigation disrupted by a maddeningly forthright beauty. Ariel Harding has her own reasons for wanting to catch the ghost. Yet when she slips into Carlton House uninvited, she never dreams she'll end up locked in a closet with an arrogant, opinionated, yet undeniably attractive scientist . . . or that she'll wind up making a perilous bargain with the very same man. They agree to exchange information—and nothing more. But neither plans on the most confounding of scientific occurrences: the breathless chemistry of desire.

"No, I do not wish to stroll with you in the garden," the girl said. "I have told you so a dozen times. I don't wish to be rude, but please go away."

The man grasped her arm, his fingers visibly digging into her flesh. He tried to pull her along with him through the crowd.

"I'll scream," said the girl, rather calmly. "I can scream very loudly. My singing teacher said I have an extraordinary set of lungs. Though an unreliable grasp of pitch," she added with regretful honesty.

Her companion ignored this threat until the girl actually opened her mouth and drew in a deep preparatory breath. Then, with a look around at the crowd and a muttered oath, he dropped her arm. "Witch," he said.

"'Double, double toil and trouble,'" she replied pertly.

The man frowned.

"'Fire, burn; and, cauldron, bubble,'" she added.

His frown became a scowl.

"Something of toad, eye of newt . . . oh, I forget the rest." She sounded merely irritated at her lapse of memory.

The man backed away a few steps.

"There's blood in it somewhere," she told herself. She made an exasperated sound. "I used to know the whole thing by heart."

Her would-be ravisher took to his heels. The girl shook out her skirts and tossed her head in satisfaction.

His interest definitely caught, Alan examined this unusual creature more closely. She was small—the top of her head did not quite reach his shoulder—but the curves of her form were not at all childlike. The bodice of her pale green gown was admirably filled and it draped a lovely line of waist and hip. Her skin glowed like ripe peaches against her glossy brown hair. He couldn't see whether her eyes had any resemblance to forest pools, but her lips were mesmerizing—very full and beautifully shaped. The word "luscious" occurred to him, and he immediately rejected it as nonsense. What the devil was he doing, he wondered? He wasn't a man to be beguiled by physical charms, or to waste his time on such maunderings. Still, he was having trouble tearing his eyes away from her when it was brought home to him that she had noticed him.

"No, I do not wish to go with you into another

room," she declared, meeting his gaze squarely. "Or into the garden, or out to your carriage. I do not require an escort home. Nor do I need someone to tell me how to go on or to 'protect' me." She stared steadily up at him, not looking at all embarrassed.

"What are you doing here?" he couldn't resist asking her.

"That is none of your affair. What are *you* doing here?"

Briefly, Alan wondered what she would think if he told her. He would enjoy hearing her response, he realized. But of course he couldn't reveal his supposed "mission."

A collective gasp passed over the crowd, moving along the room like wind across a field of grain. Alan turned quickly. This was what he had been waiting for through the interminable hours and days. There! He started toward the sweeping staircase that adorned the far end of the long room, pushing past knots of guests transfixed by the figure that stood in the shadows atop it.

On the large landing at the head of the stairs the candles had gone out—or been blown out, Alan amended. In the resulting pool of darkness, floating above the sea of light in the room, was a figure out of some sensational tale. It was a woman, her skin bone-white, her hair a deep chestnut. She wore an antique gown of yellow brocade, the neck square cut, the bodice tight above a long full skirt. Alan knew, because he had been told, that this invariably was her dress when she appeared, and that it was the costume she had worn onstage to play Lady Macbeth.

Sound reverberated through the room—the clanking of chains—as Alan pushed past the guests, who remained riveted by the vision before them. The figure seemed to hover a foot or so above the floor. The space between the hem of its gown and the stair landing was a dark vacancy. Its eyes were open, glassy and fixed, effectively dead-looking. Its hands and arms were stained with gore.

A bloodcurdling scream echoed down the stairs. Then a wavering, curiously guttural voice pronounced the word "justice" very slowly, three times. The figure's mouth had not moved during any of this, Alan noted.

He had nearly reached the foot of the stairs when a female guest just in front of him threw up her arms and crumpled to the floor in a faint. Alan had to swerve and slow to keep from stepping on her, and as he did so, something struck him from behind, upsetting his balance and nearly knocking him down. "What the devil?" he said, catching himself and moving on even as he cast a glance over his shoulder. To his astonishment, he found that the girl he had encountered a moment ago was right on his heels. He didn't have time to wonder what she thought she was doing. "Stay out of my way," he commanded, and lunged for the stairs.

In one of the most original and stunning hardcover debuts of the season, Glenna McReynolds brings historical romance readers the experience they've been waiting for: a novel of dark magic, stirring drama, and fierce passion that weaves a wondrous, unbreakable spell . . .

THE CHALICE
AND THE BLADE
BY GLENNA MCREYNOLDS

The place is twelfth-century Wales, a land of forbidding castles and ferocious knights, sacred prophesies and unholy betrayals. Deep in the caverns below the towers of Carn Merioneth, dragon nests await the arrival of one who holds the key to an ancient legacy. She is Ceridwen, daughter of a Druid priestess, unaware of her immense power—until fate leads her to a feared sorcerer. Dain Lavrans knows he has no magic, only the secrets of medicine he uncovered in the Crusades. But with the appearance of Ceridwen, he will finally behold true—and terrifying—magic, for there are many who seek to use the maiden to unlock the mystery of the dragons. Now a battle of epic proportion is about to take place. At its center stand Ceridwen and Dain, struggling to escape the snares set by friend and foe alike, while discovering that neither can resist the love that promises to bind them forever.

On sale in October:

FINDING LAURA
by Kay Hooper

HAWK O'TOOLE'S HOSTAGE
by Sandra Brown

IT HAPPENED ONE NIGHT
by Leslie LaFoy

DON'T MISS THESE FABULOUS
BANTAM WOMEN'S FICTION TITLES